"Did you hear it? Did you hear him?"

"Hear what?" Blanca asked.

"He was here. I heard him," Tate said. "I wasn't dreaming it this time."

"Dreaming what, Tate?"

"The whistling. I heard the whistling. The same song."

Blanca stared past him at the lone tree in the center of the clearing. This was it. This was the tree where Tate had been tied up.

"A-are you sure?"

"You don't believe me? I'm sure, Blanca."

"I believe you, but why? Why would he come back to this spot with you here?"

"What does it matter if I remember? I didn't see him. I can't ID him. That's clear, or he would've taken care of me years ago."

"You think he'd be worried about you catching him whistling alone in the forest? If he is the one who stole the case files from my hotel room, he knows you heard whistling."

"Maybe he didn't even know I was here. Maybe he's out trolling for another victim. That's his precursor. His warning. The whistling."

POINT OF DISAPPEARANCE

CAROL ERICSON

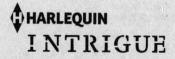

HARLEQUIN

INTRIGUE

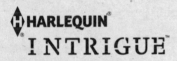

Recycling programs
for this product may
not exist in your area.

ISBN-13: 978-1-335-59135-7

Point of Disappearance

Copyright © 2023 by Carol Ericson

For questions and comments about the quality of this book,
please contact us at CustomerService@Harlequin.com.

Harlequin Enterprises ULC
22 Adelaide St. West, 41st Floor
Toronto, Ontario M5H 4E3, Canada
www.Harlequin.com

Printed in U.S.A.

Carol Ericson is a bestselling, award-winning author of more than forty books. She has an eerie fascination for true-crime stories, a love of film noir and a weakness for reality TV, all of which fuel her imagination to create her own tales of murder, mayhem and mystery. To find out more about Carol and her current projects, please visit her website at www.carolericson.com, "where romance flirts with danger."

Books by Carol Ericson

Harlequin Intrigue

A Discovery Bay Novel

Misty Hollow Massacre
Point of Disappearance

The Lost Girls

Canyon Crime Scene
Lakeside Mystery
Dockside Danger
Malice at the Marina

A Kyra and Jake Investigation

The Setup
The Decoy
The Bait
The Trap

Visit the Author Profile page at Harlequin.com.

CAST OF CHARACTERS

Tate Mitchell—A US forestry agent who uncovers bones in a shallow grave is forced to relive the nineteen-year-old nightmare of when his best friend disappeared. Can an FBI agent looking into the cold case help him expunge his guilt, or will his attraction to her only add to it?

Blanca Lopez—An FBI special agent assigned to the cold case of a missing thirteen-year-old boy, she has questions for the boy's surviving friend, but that friend, now a grown man, is proving to be a distraction from the case she needs to solve to put her career back on track.

Jeremy Ruesler—This boy went missing nineteen years ago, but the discovery of a set of bones and another missing boy might resolve his cold case.

Noah Fielding—His disappearance bears eerie similarities to Jeremy's case almost twenty years ago. Is the predator back?

Porter Monroe—This local has always been interested in the youth of Dead Falls, but now his interest suggests something sinister behind the friendly face.

The Whistler—The mystery man who may be responsible for the disappearances of both Jeremy and Noah, or has Tate imagined him?

Chapter One

The smoke unfurled like a suffocating blanket, obscuring Tate's view of the green pines in the distance. Despite the damp weather, sweat ran down his back beneath his fire shirt, which clung to him like a second skin. He hoisted his ax and buried it into a smoldering log.

The fire had already rushed through this area, but his hand crew wanted to make sure nothing reignited as the helicopters dumped flame retardant on the blaze, shifting to the right with the wind. He kicked at some blackened logs with the toe of his boot, and a flurry of sparks scattered in the air.

Turning around, he pulled the N95 mask away from his face. "I think we're almost finished with this area. The rain should be helping us out soon."

As if on cue, the skies opened, and a torrent of water pummeled the December forest fire, sending plumes of dark gray smoke billowing upward to meet the clouds. The sudden onslaught of rain turned the ashy ground beneath Tate's feet to mush.

His teammates whooped and hollered behind him,

the wait for the storm break finally over, making their job easier.

Tate yelled over his shoulder. "We're not done yet, boys. Let's break up a few more of these fallen logs. Plenty are still live."

To emphasize his point, Tate hoisted his pick ax over his head and brought it down on a smoldering stump. It hissed at him, as the rain soaked the wood, dampening the embers.

As Tate kicked at a few more logs with the toe of his heavy boot, the ground gave way beneath his other foot. He slid down an incline to the amusement of his crew.

Rivulets of water rushed past him, pooling into a muddy dip in the land. He grunted and propped himself up on his elbows, surveying the scorched trees before him.

As he scrambled to his knees they sunk in the soft earth, and he pitched forward. He thrust out a hand. It landed on a smooth rock, and he pushed against the solid object to gain some purchase.

The rock moved beneath his palm, shifting to the side. The eye sockets of a skull stared back at him. Choking, he snatched his hand back.

Like a faint echo, his teammates' voices swirled through the roaring in his ears. He licked his lips, his tongue sweeping through the wet ash clinging to his mouth.

"How long are you gonna stay down there wallowing in the mud, Tate? C'mon, man. It's almost quittin' time."

A twig cracked behind him, and Tate twisted around. "Stay where you are. We have a crime scene here."

James Clugston, his second-in-command, snorted. "What the hell are you talking about? The crime scene is where this firebug lit this blaze. We'll find it, but this ain't it."

Tate struggled to his feet, his legs rubbery. One arm windmilled for balance, as he planted his boots in the muck. "I found a skeleton down here, so I guess we have two crime scenes."

The whooping and hollering stopped, and James coughed and spit. "Are you kidding me? How old is it?"

Turning his back on the bones, Tate faced his teammates and took a deep breath, tasting the smoke from the fire on the back of his tongue. "What the hell do I look like, a medical examiner?"

"You look like a tired, overworked US Forest Service agent. Like I'm looking in the mirror." Aaron Huang stepped aside as Tate slogged up the incline.

James stood on a fallen, blackened log and peered down the gully. "Who are we calling for this? Dead Falls Sheriff's Department? I'm sure they'll be able to crack the case in about fifty years."

Despite Tate's agreement that the Dead Falls Sheriff's Department was useless, his crew's laughter rubbed him the wrong way. He snapped. "Have some respect. That's someone's kid."

Aaron choked. "Kid? That's a kid's skeleton down there? I thought you didn't know crap about forensics."

Tate gulped. Was it a kid's skeleton? Did the skull seem small? "I—I just mean, that's someone's family member. I don't know the age or the sex or anything else, but we'd better call someone who can figure that out before we trample all over everything."

Cocking his head, James said, "Haven't we already done that? We just put out a major fire on top of this crime scene."

"As incompetent as he is, we need to start with Sheriff Hopkins." Tate unzipped his vest and dug in his pocket for his cell phone.

His thumb quivered as it hovered over the numbers on the display. Was Hopkins too inept to handle the discovery of these bones? One part of Tate hoped so. He wasn't sure he wanted to know the identity of the person in that shallow grave.

BLANCA LOPEZ STEPPED off the ferry from Seattle to Dead Falls Island, rolling her suitcase beside her and clamping her laptop bag between her arm and her body. Her heels clicked authoritatively on the concrete dock, even though she hadn't a clue where she was going.

The words of her mentor, Manny Rodriguez, pinged in her brain. *Always act like you know what you're doing and where you're going.* Even though she now despised Manny, he had gotten a few things right.

She mumbled, "Got it, Manny."

"Ah, miss, er, ma'am?"

She spun around so quickly her heel caught in a crack in the concrete and she stumbled. The young deputy caught her arm, a sea of red suffusing his baby face. "Yeah, sorry."

She flicked her ponytail over her shoulder and straightened her shoulders. "No need to apologize, Deputy. You saved me from an embarrassing start to my assignment."

Dropping her arm, he said, "I'm Deputy Fletcher."

Blanca thrust out her hand. "Good to meet you, Deputy Fletcher. I'm FBI Special Agent Blanca Lopez."

When he took her hand, she squeezed hard to make up for her earlier klutziness. Had Manny ever fallen on his face when meeting the local law?

When she ended the handshake, Fletcher flexed his fingers and said, "Do you want me to take you to your hotel or straight to the station? We have a car for you at the station."

"I think station." She jiggled the handle of her suitcase. "I can dump my stuff in the car, maybe have a quick meeting with Sheriff Hopkins and pick up any files he has for me."

"Sounds good, ma'am. Can I take your bags for you?"

Blanca wrinkled her nose. "You can call me Agent Lopez, Deputy, and I can handle my own bags."

"Sure, ma— Agent Lopez." He strode ahead of her, his back stiff. "This way to the car."

Blanca bit her lip. Manny always told her to command respect, but she didn't want to get off on the wrong foot with the locals. Manny never seemed to care about local law enforcement, but Blanca had come to realize it helped the investigation if they didn't hate you. Manny wasn't always right.

She cleared her throat. "The island looked beautiful coming in on the ferry. So green. Are the falls dead? Is that the reason for the name?"

"Dead?" Fletcher cranked his gaze over his shoulder and raised his eyebrows. "Not sure what a dead waterfall would look like, but no. It's called Dead Falls because the angle on that water is a dead drop. Get it?"

"Makes sense." A lot more sense than a dead waterfall. What was a dead waterfall?

Her high heels wobbled on a pebble in the parking lot, and she took a little hopping step to avoid further embarrassment.

She eyed the suitcase trundling beside her over the rough asphalt. She'd filled it with similar work clothes—skirts, slacks, jackets, blouses and heels. She just hoped her new hiking boots would work out here and that she'd packed enough jeans and sweaters to last for the duration of her stay, and that depended on how much information the Dead Falls Sheriff's Department had on her cold case.

Maybe that fire a few days ago had already done her work for her. Case closed if the bones exposed by that blaze belonged to Jeremy Ruesler...or at least that part of the case solved. They could put Jeremy down as a murder instead of a missing child, but most law enforcement agencies and probably the poor boy's family already knew that.

If that skeleton did belong to Jeremy, they still

needed to figure out who killed him—and she had a perfect starting point for that.

Fletcher pointed out a few landmarks on their drive from the dock to the station. The rugged terrain of the island that she'd spied from the ferry spread inland, covered by dense forest and rushing bodies of water, including those falls. She'd never been much of an outdoorsy girl, but the sight of that deep green and the smell of pine mingling with the salt of the ocean had caused prickles to rush across her skin. The atmosphere of the island charged her with a sense of awakening, a new start, and she sat on the edge of the passenger seat, drinking in Fletcher's impromptu guided tour. God knew she needed a new start.

By the time the deputy pulled into the parking lot of the Dead Falls Sheriff's Station, Blanca's newfound appreciation of the world hit reality. The beige, one-story stucco building looked like police stations all across the country. She had a hard time believing the course of her future resided within those prosaic walls, but she *had* turned a corner this past year, and this assignment was going to be the culmination of her reset.

She could almost hear Manny's low laugh in her ear. *Follow me, kid, and I'll steer you right.*

She curled her fingers around the strap of her purse. Manny had steered her straight to hell. Maybe the fresh air of Dead Falls Island could blow his memory right out of her mind.

"Agent Lopez?" Fletcher sat beside her, his door

open, one foot already planted on the parking lot. "This is it."

"That didn't take long. Thanks for the guided tour." She flashed him a quick smile before releasing her seat belt and pulling the handle of the door.

The deputy waited for her at the entrance of the station and held open the door for her. "Would you like me to transfer your suitcase to the trunk of your car, Agent Lopez?"

"Whatever's most convenient for you, Deputy Fletcher."

"That way, when you're done talking to Sheriff Hopkins, I can just hand you the keys to the car and you can be on your way. There's a GPS in the car, so you can follow that to your hotel."

"That works for me. Thanks." She walked through the swinging door he held open for her and followed him down a short hallway. Her heel taps echoed in the mostly empty station. All patrol cars must be out on duty. These small stations definitely didn't have the same buzz as their big-city counterparts. The fact that they couldn't handle homicide investigations didn't surprise her. It had been a PI and a forensic psychologist who had solved the latest murder in Dead Falls. No wonder they'd had this cold case on the books for the past nineteen years.

The clicking of fingers on a keyboard intensified as they drew closer to the end of the hallway. Deputy Fletcher tapped on an open door, and the clicking stopped.

"Sheriff Hopkins, I have FBI Special Agent Blanca Lopez with me."

Blanca peeked around the corner of the office door, and a balding man with crumbs on the chest of his uniform stood up behind the desk. "Thanks, Fletch. Agent Lopez, welcome to Dead Falls Island. C'mon in. Car ready, Fletch?"

"Yes, sir. I'm just going to move Agent Lopez's suitcase from the squad car to the sedan…and the other stuff." Fletcher backed out of the sheriff's office awkwardly, his long legs almost not up to the intricate maneuver.

Blanca thanked the deputy again and stepped into Hopkins's office. Family pictures populated the bookshelf behind his desk, and plaques and awards dotted the wall. Her gaze tracked across his messy workspace, noting the absence of anything that looked like cold-case files.

Clearing her throat, she reached over the desk to shake hands. She didn't give this one the death squeeze, as his hand lay limp and damp in her own. When they broke apart, she resisted the urge to wipe her palm on her slacks.

She shuffled back, and when the back of her knees touched the edge of the chair, she sat. "Thanks for having me here, Sheriff Hopkins."

Smiling, he folded hands. "When the FBI calls and tells you they want to look into one of your cold cases, you jump."

"We appreciate the response." She settled her laptop case on the floor. "I'm assuming you haven't gotten any DNA results back from the bones, yet?"

"Nope." He transferred a batch of papers from one side of his desk to the other. "We don't have the familial DNA yet for comparison."

She widened her eyes. Were the locals just waiting for the FBI to do all the work? "Is the Ruesler family still on the island?"

"The mother is. She's not being particularly co-operative. Never was, after the initial investigation failed to locate her boy." Hopkins finally folded his hands as if to keep them from fidgeting among the mess on his desk.

"I would think…" Blanca rubbed her chin. "No, I take that back. Maybe she doesn't want to know. Some people would prefer to have that closure, and some would rather keep believing."

Hopkins lifted his rounded shoulders, spreading his hands, as if he'd never even considered the matter. "Maybe as an outsider, you can get her DNA."

"I'll try." She bent forward to retrieve a notebook and pen from the side of her bag, her ponytail slipping over her shoulder. "Is there anything you can tell me about the site where the skeleton was found? Any items there beside the bones?"

His rather dull eyes, a muddy gray, stared at her. He blinked once. "I wasn't there. US Forest Service Agent Tate Mitchell found the remains while wrapping up a forest fire."

Blanca gripped the arms of her chair, as a zing

shot up her spine. Tate Mitchell found the remains? How had she missed that all-important detail?

"Tate Mitchell? You mean the one…?"

Hopkins nodded. "Yep. Strange, isn't it?"

Strange and fortuitous at the same time. Anxious to end her pointless interview with Hopkins and start the real investigation, she shoved the notebook back in her bag, her hand hovering over the strap. "The files. Do you have the cold-case files?"

Hopkins sat back in his chair, his hands folded over his paunch, a satisfied smile on his lips. "I asked Fletcher earlier to put them in the trunk of the car we're loaning you for your stay. You'll find them next to your luggage, most likely."

"Perfect." She sprang up from the chair, hauling her bag with her. "Thanks for your time."

Hopkins nodded, a look of relief spreading across his face as he eyed the half-eaten sandwich on his desk. "Anything we can do for you, just ask."

Blanca hoisted her bag over her shoulder and stopped at the door. "One more thing."

Hopkins's hand paused, halfway to his sandwich. "Yes?"

"Do you know where I can find Tate Mitchell?"

After Hopkins scribbled down directions to Mitchell's cabin, Blanca clutched the piece of paper in her hand and strode from the station. As she pushed through the glass door, a fat drop of rain plonked on the back of her hand.

She glanced at the darkening skies. Something had to keep this island green.

Deputy Fletcher emerged from a dark sedan and waved. "I got your car, Agent Lopez. Suitcase in the trunk."

Taking a zigzag path as if she could avoid the scattered rain, she navigated to the open driver's-side door. "Thanks, Deputy. Ruesler case files?"

"In the trunk with your suitcase." He dropped the key fob in her hand. "Ma'am, you can call me Fletch. Everyone does."

"Okay, Fletch, and you can call me Blanca. Just anything besides *ma'am*." She curled her fist around the fob and ducked into the car. To hell with Manny's rules of conduct. Where had they ever got her?

She tucked the key fob into her purse on the passenger seat and punched the ignition button with her knuckle. The sedan's engine purred to life. At least they hadn't saddled her with a junker.

She smoothed the crumpled piece of paper with Mitchell's address on the console and tapped in the name of the road on the GPS. The cabin didn't have an actual house number to enter, but the GPS should get her to the general location, and then she could rely on Hopkins's directions.

Hunching over the steering wheel, she peered at the sky through the windshield. As far as she could tell, no forest fires were currently consuming the island, so Mitchell should be around and available. What were the odds that Tate Mitchell had been the one to find those bones? He must have something buried in his memory—and she was going to find out what it was.

The journey from the station took her on a windy road that ended in the town, but she took the bypass. After a few miles, the coastline and Discovery Bay disappeared as she wound her way inland, getting sucked into the emerald landscape. She'd figured it would be gray and dull out here at this time of year, but the vibrant blue of the bay and lush green of the forest dazzled her vision.

The rain had stopped by the time she made her way to Mitchell's cabin. She rolled up behind a Jeep, the tires of the sedan crunching over dirt and gravel. The *cabin* label hardly gave this abode justice.

The log exterior and Alpine roof screamed cabin, but the deck running the length of the house and the massive windows that had to afford views of the forest and bay beyond gave off luxury-resort vibes. Once again, she got the feeling of her chest expanding and her pores opening.

As she cut the engine, a tall blonde woman exited the structure, dragging a suitcase, a boy trailing behind her, a backpack slung over one shoulder. Uh-oh, had she stumbled on the Mitchell family leaving for a vacation? Maybe a Christmas vacation?

Blanca shoved open the car door, her high heel landing on the uneven ground. She should've changed before coming out here, but then maybe she would've missed the Mitchells completely.

The woman parked the suitcase on the driveway and called over her shoulder. "It's okay. The car's already here."

Blanca opened her mouth to protest when the

woman's head whipped around, her long, blond hair cascading over one shoulder. Tate Mitchell's luck must've changed somewhere along the line: he had a beautiful wife, cute son, gorgeous home and exciting job. Jeremy Ruesler was just dead.

"Go on, Olly. You can put our bags in the trunk yourself. Don't make the driver do it." The woman nudged the boy while flashing her pearly whites at Blanca.

A man clumped down the steps of the house behind the woman and child. "I told you I'd drive you, Astrid."

Blanca kept her jaw firmly in place as she eyed the tall Nordic-looking man dressed like a lumberjack in jeans, boots and a blue-plaid flannel shirt. Tate Mitchell had lucked out in the looks department, too. He resembled a modern-day Thor. All he needed was a giant square hammer over his shoulder.

So, Thor wasn't going with his wife and child. She'd lucked out, too.

The boy, Olly, grabbed his mother's suitcase and dragged it behind him as he trundled toward Blanca. "C-can I put this in the back, please?"

Blanca waved her hands. "I'm so sorry for the confusion. I'm not your driver."

"I didn't think so." Mitchell drew up beside his statuesque wife and hung his arm around her shoulders, but his gaze flicked from Blanca's ponytail, which was now frizzing in the moisture, to the tips of her high heels. Her toes curled in the very shoes under his scrutiny, and a little ball of fury formed in her gut at his assessing stare. Men shouldn't eye other women like that in the presence of their families.

The rattle of an engine behind her took away Mitchell's focus as he leveled a finger at the small car. "That must be your ride. Is the car even big enough for your bag?"

"Stop worrying." Astrid placed two hands on his broad chest and shoved. Then she gave Blanca another smile that made her skin glow even more. "My apologies for the mistake."

"No worries." Blanca held up her hands. "I'm actually here to see Tate Mitchell."

"That would be him." Astrid jerked her thumb toward her husband. "Olly, put the bags in the car."

Both she and her husband followed the boy to the car. A young man jumped out and took the suitcase from him. "I got this, my man."

With Olly settled in the back seat, Astrid turned to Tate and gave him a kiss on the cheek. "Don't forget to join us for the holiday. I'll text you from Mom's."

If her husband seemed disappointed in the chaste farewell, he didn't show it. Hunching his shoulder, Tate shoved his hands in his pockets and watched the car turn in the driveway.

Then he faced her and raised his eyebrows over a pair of eyes so blue they could've been drops from Discovery Bay. "I suppose you're here about the bones. Hopkins call you in from Seattle?"

Blanca squared her shoulders. "I'm FBI Special Agent Blanca Lopez, Mr. Mitchell. I'm here to investigate the cold case of Jeremy Ruesler. And I want to start my investigation by asking you what you remember about the day you two were playing in the forest and authorities found you tied to a tree with blood in your shoes…and no sign of Jeremy."

Chapter Two

Tate swallowed hard, the hands in his pockets curling into fists. He knew this day would come. He should've known it would as soon as he discovered those bones in the ash of the forest fire. What he didn't expect was the accusatory tone of the FBI agent in charge of the investigation…at least not right out of the box. She seemed angry with him.

He cleared his throat and glanced at the morose sky, his gaze meandering to the agent's olive-green pantsuit, her pale-yellow blouse, open to reveal the tan, slim column of her neck and settling on her high heels rapidly sinking into the dirt. "It's probably going to start raining in earnest. Let's take this inside."

He shifted to the right to allow her to walk ahead of him. Her heels wobbled on the driveway, and he resisted the urge to place a hand on her hip to steady her. She managed to make it to the porch without stumbling and climbed the two steps to the wooden deck.

As he reached past her to open the front door, her heel must've caught in a groove in the wood, and she tripped. This time he grabbed her arm. "If you're planning to stick around, you need to get yourself a different pair of shoes."

She glanced at his hand still on her sleeve and ran her tongue along her pillowy bottom lip. "I figured that out already. I'm still in my work clothes from the office, but I brought more appropriate attire."

He released his grip and patted the wrinkled material of her suit jacket. "Sorry about that. C'mon in."

He beckoned to her as he took a few steps down to the great room, one glass wall facing the forest, the stone fireplace cold for now.

Her dark eyes widened. "This is a beautiful room. It's like you're in the middle of the forest."

Cocking his head, he said, "I guess so. Would you like something to drink? Coffee? Tea? Water?"

"Tea would be nice, thanks."

He moved toward the kitchen, and she parked herself on one of the stools at the island. She dragged a notebook from her expensive-looking leather satchel and plopped it on the granite countertop. She lined up her cell phone next to the notepad. "Do you mind if I record our conversation?"

He jerked his hand, and the water filling the teapot splashed his fingers. "I guess not, but I'm afraid you're in for a disappointment. I don't remember what occurred that day. I've been to hypnotists and therapists, and whatever happened is buried deep."

She tapped the display on her phone and adjusted its position on the swirling green granite. "I had read that, but maybe with the discovery of those bones—

your discovery of the bones—something might click in your brain."

He set the kettle on the burner and turned toward her, folding his arms. "Forensics isn't back, yet. We don't even know if those bones belong to Jeremy."

"Did you find them near where he went missing nineteen years ago?"

"No." He rubbed his eye. He and Jeremy had never played on that side of the island. Too dangerous, their parents had said.

He grabbed a mug from the cupboard and a stash of several different tea bags Astrid liked. He held them up to Lopez. "Anything catch your fancy?"

"Anything herbal is fine."

Holding the selection up to his face, he squinted at the print and selected one with orange and cinnamon. A few minutes later, the kettle started whistling, and he ripped open the packet and hung the string of the tea bag over the edge of the cup while he poured the hot water over it. Steam rose from the cup, the smell of the cinnamon with it.

He placed the cup in front of Lopez. "My sister drinks this one a lot. I recognize the smell."

"Your sister?" She dredged the bag in the water, raising her eyes to his face.

"That stubborn blonde you met earlier. That's my sister, Astrid, and her son, Olly. They've been staying with me temporarily since my sister…uh, had some problems." He shrugged. "I told her I'd take her to the ferry to Seattle where she was catching a flight to Florida to visit our mother, but she didn't want to put me out."

"Oh, your sister." Lopez's shoulders rounded and she released a long breath. "I thought that was your wife."

"God, no." He laughed and smacked his forehead.

"And your wife doesn't mind sharing her home with your sister?" She cranked her head back and forth as if expecting this wife to pop out of the woodwork at any time. Why was she so insistent on him having a wife?

"She might mind if I had one. A wife, I mean." He held up his left hand as if he felt he needed to show her proof of his marital status. "Single."

Lopez's gaze slid to her phone, still recording their every word, and a blush tinted her cheeks beneath her tanned skin. She picked up the phone by its edges, and her thumb grazed the screen.

Had she thought better of exposing their conversation to other ears? It's not like asking about his marital status was unprofessional, but she must've felt the underlying tension to their dialogue, too.

He pointed a finger at the tea bag still swirling in her cup. "I'll get you a plate for that."

When he turned back around, small plate in hand, Lopez had regained her composure. Her pen moved across the notebook in a fluid script, as her short, polished nails gleamed under the pendant lights hanging above the island.

She thanked him for the plate and then said, "Tell me everything you remember about that day with

Jeremy Ruesler. Did you notice anyone following you? Anyone suspicious? Strangers in the area?"

Spreading his hands, he said, "I'm sure this is all in the case files, and my statements back then would've been fresher than anything I can give you today. Have you read the case files, yet?"

"I read what the special agent in charge gave me when he assigned this case to me." She jerked a thumb over her shoulder. "The case files from the Dead Falls Sheriff's Department are in the trunk of my car. I haven't gone through them yet."

"Maybe you should do that first and then follow up with me." Despite his words, a knot formed in his gut at the thought of this woman peering at him as a child through the lens of the present. Not that he'd done anything wrong. He hadn't done anything wrong.

"I thought it would be more helpful to question you now, as an adult. Find out if any of those memories have surfaced. You were a boy then, traumatized, in shock." She peered at him over the rim of her cup as she took a sip of tea.

Her brown eyes skewered him, as if she could read his mind. As if she knew on some level that the event still traumatized him. His parents had sent him to a therapist after Jeremy's disappearance, but he hadn't talked to her much. Law enforcement at the time had even tried hypnosis, but he hadn't been susceptible. He'd never been able to go back to that time and remember. Why did Agent Lopez believe he could do it now?

She asked in a soft voice. "Can we try?"

"Why not?" He circled the island and dragged a stool from beneath the counter overhang. He sat down, facing her, his knees almost touching the side of her stool.

He remembered his first interview after the deputies found him tied to a tree. He'd spoken to Sheriff Maddox at the time, and even though a female deputy had sat in on the interview, Tate had been scared to death.

As he watched Agent Lopez scoot her stool around so that she faced him, her knees inches from his, her curvy figure visible as her jacket gaped open, he figured she could probably get a lot more out of him than gruff Maddox and the dour-faced female deputy.

She cleared her throat and tugged her jacket closed. "What kind of day was it? Did you and Jeremy always play together in the woods?"

"It was after Christmas. We were still on winter break from school, so probably about three weeks from today's date. Jeremy had a new bike, so of course we were going to go out riding in the forest. He was my best friend." Tate's nose tingled, but he didn't dare sniff. "Harry van Pelt also hung out with us, but he was sick that week."

"You always rode your bikes in the forest? People would know that?"

"Sure, yeah. A lot of the kids did. We were twelve at the time, so, uh, we were kind of coming to the end of our childhood. Boys a year ahead of us were already hanging out by the falls, teasing the girls."

A smile tugged at his lips as he remembered how conflicted he, Jeremy and Harry were about girls.

"What time of day was it?"

"Late afternoon, but not dark yet. Our parents always gave us the directive to be home before dark. We took it seriously because our parents would ground us if we broke curfew." He rubbed his chin as he stared over her shoulder. "This island can be a dangerous place, Agent Lopez."

"Call me Blanca, please." She flicked her slim fingers in the air. "Was there a particular game you played, or did you just ride your bikes through the woods?"

"We'd ride and do some stunts like hop over logs or skid sideways down an incline. Honestly, we were pretending to be motocross riders." He put a finger to his lips. "But don't tell anyone that. We never did."

"You never told the police that?" She tilted her head and her ponytail, which had curled at the ends, danced on her shoulder.

"That's not a big deal, is it? Kids' make-believe?" He drummed his fingers on the table. Did Blanca think she'd just coaxed him into a breakthrough?

"Probably not, but it means you didn't tell the deputies everything. You held back. Makes me wonder what else you didn't disclose." She wrapped her ponytail around her hand before tossing it over her shoulder. "So you and Jeremy were playing motocross in the forest in the late afternoon. What's the last thing you remember before coming to, tied to the tree?"

"I just remember the playing. Nothing happened. Nobody approached us. Neither of us got hurt or…" He stopped and chewed on his bottom lip.

"Or what?" She shimmied up to the edge of the stool, her knee bumping his. "Did one of you crash, fall, get hurt?"

He nodded. "I did hit a log and crash, and there was blood in my shoes. The bottoms of my feet and my socks were ripped up, like I'd been running without my shoes. But that makes no sense to me. I don't have any recollection of taking off my shoes or running without them."

"It was your blood, not Jeremy's."

"That's correct." He clenched the edges of the stool with both hands. "I didn't have any of Jeremy's blood on me."

He released the chair and flexed his fingers. Had Blanca noticed the defensive hysteria in his voice?

Her luminous eyes studied his face, and the look she gave him caused a lump to form in his throat and made him feel like crying, something he'd never done as a shell-shocked twelve-year-old.

Her hand grazed his leg as she resettled herself in her seat. "In fact, Jeremy's blood wasn't found at the scene, was it?"

"They didn't find anything of Jeremy's, except his new bike and his Linkin Park hat. There was nothing in the hat. No other DNA except Jeremy's, no blood, no sign of trauma to the hat."

She asked, "Was the hat found near the bike?"

"It was."

"But not near where you were located." She crossed one leg over the other and clasped her hands over her knee. "What did you remember when you woke up against that tree? Had you come to before the deputies found you?"

"I didn't remember a thing. I was out until the deputies discovered me. They called my name and started untying me. I panicked." He scooped in a deep breath. "I thought maybe Jeremy and I had been playing some other sort of game and he tied me up. I didn't even know Jeremy was missing until they all started asking me where he was. His mother. Everybody. *Where's Jeremy?*"

He must've drifted off because Blanca touched his leg, on purpose this time.

"That must've been terrifying. And you could never remember what happened out there." She clicked her nails on the granite. "You said they tried hypnosis?"

"I'm not a good subject." He drew back his shoulders as if that fact made him proud. Did it? If he were a good subject, he could've helped solve Jeremy's disappearance. Could've given Mrs. Ruesler some answers.

"Have you tried lately?"

Tate's jaw dropped. "Now? How would that even be reliable after nineteen years?"

"That's the point of hypnosis. It's revealing memories that occurred in the past, undiluted by time and other impressions." Blanca scribbled some words in the notebook and flipped it shut.

"Is it, though? Can't hypnosis plant memories?" He pushed back from the stool and stood up. If she was done with him, he didn't want to encourage her to continue. He'd had enough.

"I suppose it can, but we've used it before to good effect."

"I think it's a certain personality type that's not responsive to hypnosis." He thumped his chest with a fist. "Not then, not now."

She raised her perfectly sculpted eyebrows. "I think it's more of a cognitive style than a personality type, but if you already strongly believe it won't work on you, then it probably won't."

"More tea?" He pinged her cup with his finger-nail, and then held his breath. He was supposed to be getting rid of her.

"I'll finish what I have." She curled her fingers around the handle of the mug and swirled the re-maining liquid. "How did you feel when you found those bones last week?"

Her words hit him like a punch to the gut. Just when he thought she'd finished with him, she had to dig deeper.

Crossing his arms, he wedged his hip against the counter. "Surprised. Distressed. I was putting out a forest fire. I didn't expect to find a shallow grave."

"It must have occurred to you that the bones could be Jeremy's." She narrowed her eyes, ready to dis-believe any lie that sprang to his lips.

With his arms still folded, he hunched his shoul-ders, closing her out. "I found bones. I didn't immediately think of Jeremy. Like I said… Blanca, Dead Falls Island is a dangerous place."

She scooted off the stool, giving a little hop to reach the floor. "I'm sure I'll have more questions after I go through the case file, Mr. Mitchell."

His lips quirked at her formality. "It's Tate. This ain't Washington, DC, Blanca."

"I gathered that." She turned to place her cup in the sink and tripped to a stop at the view outside the windows in the great room. "It's dark already."

"Well, it is winter. Or almost." He took the cup from her grasp, his fingers brushing the soft skin on the back of her hand. He didn't see a ring on her finger, either. He hadn't had a girlfriend in the longest time and enjoyed playing the field, but he drew the line at married women. He hoped he didn't have to draw any lines with Blanca Lopez.

She smoothed her slacks over her rounded hips and tugged at the hem of her jacket. "Are you going to be joining your sister soon at your mother's place, or will you be around for a while?"

"I'll be here for a while. You?"

"Until I solve this cold case." She flattened her lush lips against her teeth and still managed to look sexy as hell.

"You may be here a long time, Blanca." He rubbed his hands together. "Do you want a jacket to go over your suit for your walk to the car? If you thought it was cold this afternoon, wait until you feel it when the sun goes down. I'm sure Astrid has something you can borrow."

"I have a raincoat in my car, thanks." As she reached for her purse on the counter, Tate's phone rang.

His pulse ticked up a few notches when he saw the incoming number of the Dead Falls Sheriff's Department. Had they IDed the bones?

He held up a finger to Blanca. "Let me get this, and then I'll walk you to the car."

He tapped the phone. "Tate Mitchell."

"Tate, it's Amanda at the station."

Frowning, he asked, "Why are you whispering, Amanda?"

"I'm not sure if I'm allowed to release this info yet, but I thought you should know."

"The bones?" He glanced at Blanca, who'd stopped digging around in her purse. "Did you get the DNA results back on the bones?"

"No, it's not that, Tate." Amanda sighed over the phone. "It's another boy. Another boy has gone missing from the island."

Chapter Three

Blanca watched Tate's handsome face lose all color, and her heart tripped. Was it the DNA? Had the medical examiner determined the bones belonged to an adolescent male? They couldn't have a match yet for Jeremy without the familial DNA to compare.

She clutched her purse to her chest as she listened to Tate on the phone.

"When?" He ran a hand through his spiky blond hair. "So he could've just wandered off. Is there a search underway?"

Blanca curled her fingers into the leather of her purse and swallowed, her throat suddenly dry. Search for whom?

Tate continued. "Okay, let me know when it starts. I'll be there. Thanks, Amanda."

When he ended the call, Tate stood frozen, the phone pressed against his chin.

Blanca took a tentative step toward him. "What was that about? Who's missing?"

Tate shook his head. "A boy. A tourist. His family was camping near Prescott River. He wandered off this morning and didn't come back for breakfast. The family reported him missing after a few hours of searching for him."

"Just this morning?" Blanca hissed out a little breath she didn't know she'd been holding. "Maybe he's lost. Maybe he had a fight with his parents and took off to make a point. That's something I probably would've done if my parents had dragged me on a camping trip in the middle of December."

"Fishing trip for Christmas break. Not too unusual, but not the height of the season by any stretch, which is why nobody saw Noah."

"Are the deputies searching for him now?" Blanca drew her bottom lip between her teeth. Would the DFSD call in the FBI if they couldn't find him? Probably not, if they believed his disappearance was an accident.

Tate answered. "They're just starting to organize a night search for him. If he's not found by tomorrow morning, the deputies will most likely launch a search from the air."

"And you're going to join the night search."

"I am." His forehead crinkled. "It's odd, isn't it?"

She knew exactly what he meant. She'd felt it, too, despite her attempt to make light of the boy's disappearance. "You mean that one week after you find those bones, another boy goes missing."

He jerked his head up, his eyes widening, as if her take surprised him. "Yeah."

"People have gone missing on the island since Jeremy, right? Kids?"

"Sure, sure. A few have even died, victims of the rough terrain." He glanced at his phone as it buzzed in his hand. "The news is going public. The sheriff's department just invited interested people to meet at the parents' campsite."

"The family isn't still there, are they?" She put a hand to her throat. She couldn't imagine their terror.

"They've been moved to a motel in town." Tate clasped the back of his neck. "I'm going to get ready now. I'll walk you out to your car first."

"I'm joining the search, too."

He dipped his head, taking in her high heels. "Uh, that foot wear ain't gonna cut it."

She silently cursed Manny's bad advice about dressing to impress. Had he purposely led her astray? "I told you I had different clothes in my suitcase. I'll change and join the search. You and I both know this might be connected to the bones."

"You just got here. You don't even know the lay-out of the island."

She shrugged. "I can head to the sheriff's department and present myself as a volunteer. I'm sure someone, maybe Fletch, will take me to the search."

"Tell you what." He smacked the countertop. "I'll get ready and then follow you to your hotel. You can change there, and we'll go over to the search together."

"Why waste time?" She dragged out the key fob to the sheriff's sedan. "My suitcase is in my trunk. I'll change here, and we can head out directly without any detours."

His mouth opened a closed a few times.

Did he find her presumptuous? They'd just met, and she was proposing she change clothes in his house. Was she overstepping?

He held out his hand. "I'll bring it in."

She placed the key fob in his palm, and he strode outside. As she watched him from the window, he popped the trunk and hoisted her hard-sided suitcase to the ground.

He stared into the trunk. He must be looking at those boxes. Had he ever read the case files as an adult? She should suggest he peruse them. If he did, he might actually remember something from that day.

As he slammed the trunk and dragged the case to the house, she jumped back from the window and pulled out her phone.

"Reporting to the home office?" He parked the suitcase at the foot of the stairs.

"Not yet." She dropped her phone in her pocket. She had no intention of telling her supervisor about this new case—not yet, anyway.

Tate aimed a toe at the suitcase. "I'll carry this upstairs. There are four bedrooms. The two on the right belong to Astrid and Olly. The main one's at the end, and there's a spare on the left. A friend of mine was staying there until recently, but I've cleaned up everything. You're welcome to change there."

"Got it."

She followed him up the stairs, noting the way his flannel shirt tightened across his back muscles as he carried her heavy suitcase. Too bad the cold weather had him all covered up.

He placed the suitcase on the floor and wheeled it into a bedroom, complete with queen-size bed, nightstands and a dresser with a mirror. "Let me know if you need any additional clothes. Astrid wouldn't mind."

Blanca smirked. "Except Astrid's about six feet tall."

"Not quite, and she's skinny." As soon as the words left his mouth, he pursed his lips.

Drawing back her shoulders, Blanca wedged a hand on her hip. "And I'm...?"

"Thin, but not as skinny as Astrid. She's a bean pole."

"Your sister looks like a supermodel. Don't insult her to save yourself." She wanted to put the poor guy out of his misery, so she laughed. "Don't worry. I'm not that sensitive about my appearance."

"And why would you be? You look—" He cleared his throat. "I'll meet you downstairs in a few."

When he shut the door behind him, she turned to the mirror. Whatever he was going to say, it wasn't that she looked ready to search the wilderness for a lost child.

She kicked off her high heels, shrugged out of her jacket and unzipped her slacks. When she finished undressing, she folded her clothes on the bed. Who'd been his recent guest? The room didn't look particularly masculine or feminine.

She pulled a pair of jeans, socks and a fuzzy red

sweater from her bag. She dressed quickly in front of the mirror and then sat on the edge of the bed to step into her new hiking boots. She hadn't had much time to wear them, but the reviews had said they didn't need much breaking in.

She clumped down the stairs, calling Tate's name. "I'm ready to go." She jumped when Tate came through the front door.

Holding up a backpack, he said, "I put some supplies together. First-aid kit, rope, extra flashlights, headlamp. That boy could in the water, stuck on a cliff or stranded in the forest."

"I hope it is one of those." She turned around in front of him. "Will this do?"

He screwed up one side of his mouth, as he inspected her outfit. "Jacket?"

She pointed to her dark green puffy coat with a fur-lined hood.

He nodded. "What do you have on underneath that sweater?"

She cocked an eyebrow at him. Was he really going there? "Umm, a bra."

"I know *that*." His gaze seemed to caress her breasts, and an excited tingle raced across her skin. "I mean, you should probably have a thermal beneath the sweater. You know, like a long underwear top."

"You think it'll get that cold?"

"It can. I'll run upstairs and get something from Astrid's room. You need a pair of gloves, too."

"I have those." Did he think she was totally unprepared? She pulled a pair of fuzzy gloves from the pocket of her jacket and dangled them in the air.

"Those will work." He turned toward the stairs. "Be right back."

She watched his backside as he took the stairs two at a time with excitement fizzing through her veins. She didn't know if the thrill came from her attraction to Tate or the thought of joining in on a search that might be related to her cold case, but she'd take either one.

Two minutes later, he came charging back down the stairs with a thin white long-sleeved shirt bunched in his hand. He tossed it toward her. "Put that on under your sweater. I'll start the Jeep. Just pull the door closed behind you when you leave. I can arm the security system from my phone."

As soon as the front door shut, she pulled her arms from the sleeves of her sweater and lifted it from her head, careful not to disturb the bun that would keep her hair from going wild in this moist air. She ducked her head into the hole of the thermal and tugged it over her body, tucking the hem into her jeans. She put her sweater back on, grabbed her jacket and clicked the front door behind her, checking that it was locked.

Her new boots crunched over the gravel of the driveway, and she marched to the passenger side of the Jeep with confidence. She hopped in beside Tate and yanked on the seat belt. "How far?"

"About twenty minutes. Gets a little rugged and

slow as we near the campsites. That's why people like them. They're always booked in the summer."

She shivered in the heated car. "I can't imagine camping in the cold like this."

He circled around the driveway, a smile quirking his lips. "Have you ever been camping before?"

"A few times." She waved her hand in the air. "There was a school trip to some cabins in Malibu."

A muffled noise came from Tate's side of the car, and Blanca decided to quit while she was ahead. "Did the deputy send you any more information?"

"Nope. Just verified that the search was still on. Sheriff Hopkins should be there. You met him, right?"

"That was my first stop when the ferry docked. Deputy Fletcher picked me up and took me to the station. Wasn't impressed."

"With the station or with Sheriff Hopkins?"

"Both. Neither." She placed two fingers against her lips. "Am I speaking out of turn here? Is he some beloved sheriff who makes everyone feel safe and cozy on the island?"

"Absolutely not. He's not elected, and the council members who appointed him already know the majority of the island wants to see a change next year. I suppose it might depend on how he handles Noah's case, maybe even Jeremy's cold case."

"Great." She smacked her knees. "You're telling me if I solve that cold case, it could keep Hopkins in his position?"

"It'll make him look good." He turned his head

and studied her face in the darkness of the car. "It'll make you look good."

"It's my job." She tapped her fingers on the glass, hoping to change the subject from her job and why the agent in charge sent her out here. "That waterfall is amazing."

"The Dead Falls from which the island gets its name. Powerful."

"Beautiful." She took a deep breath. Even the air in the car smelled better than car air in DC. "We're crossing the bridge?"

"The area across the bridge is called Misty Hollow due to the spray from the falls. A Samish Indian reservation is on this side, also, and then the campsites. The Indian nation owns the campsite, but the Dead Falls Sheriff's Department provides the law enforcement."

Blanca placed a palm on the cold glass as they crossed the bridge, the rushing water of the falls to her right. "I hope Noah is okay. Could he have come this far to the falls?"

"It's possible." He tipped his head toward her window. "There are caves behind the falls, and Dead Falls teens have been creeping back there for years. I'm sure Noah would've known about the falls if his parents had any tourist brochures about the area lying around, but maybe not about those caves."

Blanca turned away from the pounding water, the images in her head making her nauseous. "Will they search the falls?"

"Someone probably already searched the caves.

The water below will have to wait until tomorrow and daylight."

Blanca pinned her hands between her bouncing knees. "It might be too late by then."

"There's only so much searching we can do at night." Tate made a sharp left turn off the bridge and flicked on the windshield wipers to take care of the fine mist that gathered on the glass.

She sat forward in her seat, the seat belt rustling against the slick material of her jacket. "This side of the island is definitely wilder than the other side."

"And more dangerous."

Tate took his vehicle down a road, and Blanca felt as if the trees had swallowed them whole. Slivers of silver sparkling streams peeked through the forest like some fairy wonderland. Maybe Noah was just enjoying his freedom. They had no idea if he were the type of boy who'd be concerned about worrying his parents.

A sign announced their entrance to the Samish Nation's area, but the reservation wasn't visible from the road. Blanca could see some taillights ahead, and she pointed. "Looks like we're not the only ones out for the search."

"There's usually a good turnout, especially for children." Tate's jaw tightened, and a small muscle ticked at the corner of his mouth. This had to be bringing back memories for him.

"Did they find you at night?"

"What?" He jerked his head to the side, a scowl

marring his face. "Yeah, they found me at night. Do you think this is going to bring it all back to me?"

Her back stiffened at the ferocity of his tone. Just because she found the man insanely attractive was no reason to back down. "It could."

"Sorry to disappoint you, Agent Lopez, but this isn't my first rodeo. I've joined searches before without any bells going off."

"I'm not excited that another child might have been snatched, if that's what you mean." She stuffed her hands in her pockets. "But you found the bones, now this. You could open your mind."

Tate slammed his hands on the steering wheel. "Is that what you think? I just haven't *opened my mind*?"

She'd blinked when his hands hit the wheel, and she decided to keep her mouth shut. Of course he'd tried to remember what had happened. Why wouldn't he want to know? Unless he felt he'd done something wrong at the time.

A glow of light appeared over the next ridge, and they soon drew close to a clutch of cars and some emergency vehicles. Her heart jumped. "Do you think they found him?"

"The ambulances are probably there for insurance, in case he's found and needs treatment or transport to the hospital. I have an app on my phone. I would've been alerted if he'd been found."

When Tate pulled to the side of the road, Blanca closed her eyes and said a silent prayer for Noah's safety.

When she opened her eyes, Tate nodded at her. "You ready?"

In answer, she shoved open the door and hopped to the ground, her boots making a satisfying crunch.

Tate led the way, and she followed him toward the crowd, a deputy calling out instructions to them.

"We're putting you in groups of six. If you have a flashlight of your own, raise it in the air. We don't have enough for everyone." The deputy pointed to Tate. "Tate, you can lead one group. Stand by the sign."

The deputy called out a few more groups leaders, but Blanca clung to Tate's sleeve. "I'm on your team."

A big burly redhead had a group of teens around him, as he gave them instructions. A mom, a worried expression on her face, gathered her family around her and handed out flashlights.

About ten minutes later, nine groups had been formed, and four people had joined her on Tate's team—a total of two women and four men. One couple introduced themselves. The man, Steven, was a fisherman and his wife, Jeanie, a nurse. One of the single men stuck his hand out to Blanca.

"Dr. Scotty Summers. Happy to work with you."

Blanca shook his hand and introduced herself by name only. "We have a doctor and a nurse. Seems like we have a good group."

He nodded toward Tate returning from a discussion with the deputies. "And Tate there knows this forest like the back of his hand."

As Tate approached the group, he scanned them with his light and reiterated the search instructions the deputy had given them. Then their group moved into the darkness, flashlights scanning the ground beneath them.

Tate turned and walked backward a few steps. "Noah was wearing blue jeans, high-top sneakers, a blue windbreaker and a black beanie with a smiley face on it. His parents don't recall what shirt he had on, but he favored black shirts with band names. Remember, if you do come across something suspicious, don't touch it. I have some gloves if you need them, but we'll call Deputy Cheswick if we do find something."

Following close on Tate's heels, Blanca aimed her flashlight at the ground, skimming over dead leaves, twigs, rocks and dirt. Tate provided a running commentary about signs that indicated a human had moved through the area.

Blanca again got the feeling that the forest was engulfing her. The pine trees on the island didn't lose their needles in winter. If anything, they created a lush landscape that looked almost impenetrable... but here they were.

In this terrain, they couldn't space out and move as one. Everyone tried to stay in a straight horizontal line, but they were separated by boulders and trees. Blanca could keep track of her teammates by the bobbing lights that would suddenly appear to her left and right.

She clambered over a log, grateful for Astrid's thermal beneath her sweater as the wind picked up and tried to blow through her.

After what seemed like hours but was most likely minutes, Blanca stopped to take a deep breath. She'd been panting as her legs cranked up and down over the uneven terrain. She could use some water and knew Tate had some in his pack.

She aimed her flashlight in front of her and saw Tate ahead, still churning through the landscape. Figuring she could backtrack over the ground between her and Tate, she picked up her pace and made a beeline for him.

When she was almost upon him, he disappeared from her view. She swept the beam of her light back and forth, and it picked him up crouched on the ground.

"Tate?" She tripped on a root and righted herself, coming up behind him, still bent forward. "Did you find something?"

He turned his head over his shoulder, squinting into her light. With a gloved hand, he picked up a dark object. "It's his. It's Noah's hat."

"His hat? That's great. Maybe he dropped it here. Is there anything else?" Her light skimmed across the dark beanie in Tate's unsteady hand, and his eyes glistened. Her heart pounded. "Tate?"

"It has blood on it."

Chapter Four

Tate held the black beanie between two gloved fingertips where it dangled in the path of Blanca's light. A dark red substance stained the smiley face on the front of the cap. The knots in his gut twisted until he couldn't breathe.

The blood could be from a fall, getting whacked in the face with a tree branch, even a wild animal. It didn't mean a predator of the human kind had gotten to Noah.

What was the name of the band on Noah's shirt? He glanced at his boots. Did he have blood in his shoes? He expanded his chest against the ropes that bound him to the tree. Had the whistling stopped?

"Tate!"

Blanca's voice pulled him back from some dark abyss where his mind was teetering. He jerked his head up to find her standing next to him, her hand on his shoulder.

"Tate, are you all right? Should I call Deputy Cheswick?"

He gulped in a deep breath and dropped the hat

where he'd found it. "Yeah, call him. They can bag it. I'm going to blow the whistle for our team. We can fan out from this spot to see if there's anything else. It doesn't look good."

Her wide-eyed gaze dropped to the hat. "It *is* good. It's a start. Noah might have fallen and cut himself. It's just a hat and a little blood."

He rose to his feet beside her. Was she trying to convince him or herself? "You call Cheswick. I'll get the rest of our team over here."

He lifted the whistle that hung around his neck to his mouth and put it between his lips. He barely had enough air in his lungs to blow. He scooped in a deep breath, and the sound of the whistle pierced the night air just as it had almost twenty years ago.

AN HOUR LATER, Tate cranked on the heat in the Jeep and leaned back against the headrest, his hands on the steering wheel. He finally felt back in control of his senses after being out in the forest in the dark with that bloody cap.

"I'll bring you back to my place, so you can pick up your bags and head to your hotel."

"If they'll still have me." Blanca rubbed her hands together in front of the vent spewing warm air. "I think it's way past check-in time."

"The island is small-town. The folks at the hotel will know exactly who you are, why you're on the island and why you haven't checked in yet." He started the car and followed a few other cars leaving the search site.

"That's kind of scary."

"Scary?" He sent a sideways glance toward Blanca, still flexing her fingers in front of the heat. "Most people find it comforting."

"*Anonymity* is comfort. I don't want people to know my business." Her lips flattened into a thin line.

"Big-city girl?"

"Born and raised in LA, attended a big state school. Kept things private. Once people know your business, they can use it against you." She tapped the window as they passed the falls again. "Are they going to search the water and rocks below the falls tomorrow?"

"As far as I know. I suppose he could've lost that hat on the way to the falls." He tightened his fingers on the steering wheel. He'd discovered the only clue tonight, the hat. They'd test the blood to see if it matched Noah's or if it was animal blood…or someone else's. Could they get that lucky?

Nineteen years ago, the blood in his shoes when they'd found him had been his own. Law enforcement hadn't discovered any other DNA on him.

"What led you to that spot tonight?" Blanca traced a seam on her jacket with the tip of her finger. "You're the only one who found anything, and you're the one who found the bones earlier in the week."

He took the turn off the bridge a little sharply, and Blanca had to grab the edge of her seat to keep from pitching to the side. "Are you implying that my subconscious led me to the bones and that cap? I hate to poke a hole in your theory, but I was fighting a forest fire when I found those bones. Any one of my crew could've discovered them. And tonight? That's where Cheswick sent our team, remember?"

"But nobody else on your team found them. And as I recall, you thrashed through the forest ahead of the rest of us like a homing beacon."

"You're kidding." He hit the steering wheel with one hand. "You're grasping at straws, Agent Lopez. Nothing led me to the location of that hat except common sense and searching techniques."

He felt her attention on his face, and he tried to keep it impassive as he remembered those flashes that had bombarded him when he'd held the cap between his fingers. The unease had started early in the search when the deputy had mentioned Noah's clothing. Jeremy favored those black band T-shirts, too—not that he believed for a minute some crazed pedophile was hell-bent on finding boys wearing band T-shirts.

He wiped a trickle of sweat from the side of his face with the heel of his hand and turned down the heat. "You warm enough now?"

"Finally. I'm glad you suggested your sister's thermal top. I think I needed that extra layer." She unzipped her jacket and flapped it over her body. "I need to ask you a favor."

"Ask away." His heart skipped a beat in his chest. Was she going to ask him to stay at his place? Maybe share his bed for warmth?

"I need you to come with me to talk to Mrs. Ruesler."

Her words socked him in the gut, and he gulped. "Talk to Mrs. Ruesler about what?"

"I need to get a DNA sample from her, and I gather up until this point she's refused." She formed her fingers into a gun and pointed it at him. "I'm thinking you can help persuade her."

Blanca had thought wrong. "Wait, why do you need her DNA? If it's just to find out if the bones I discovered belong to Jeremy, why not use the DNA you have on Jeremy?"

"Funny thing happened on the way to the lab." She rolled her eyes in an exaggerated manner. "The DNA sample we had for Jeremy is corrupted. Apparently, some genius stored it when it was still damp and bacteria has grown in the container and destroyed the DNA."

Thunking his forehead with his fist, Tate said, "Unbelievable."

"I know, right? But it's okay. Mrs. Ruesler is still in the area, and we can see if there's a match between the DNA extracted from the bones and hers. We can get enough of a relational match to verify the bones belong to Jeremy." Blanca twisted in her seat. "She is the only family still here, right?"

"She and Mr. Ruesler divorced about a year after Jeremy's disappearance, and when Jeremy's sister Celine graduated from high school a few years later, she left. I think she's married and living in Idaho. I don't know why Mrs. Ruesler stays here." Tate blinked and swallowed a lump in his throat.

Blanca said, "I know why she stays here."

Tate flicked on his high beams as he turned down the road to his cabin. "Because she's waiting for Jeremy to return."

"Exactly." Blanca sniffed and patted the end of her nose. "Sad, isn't it? Maybe if we can ID Jeremy, it might give her permission to leave."

Tate pulled in beside Blanca's sedan. "I'll load your suitcase back in your car. Do you want me to follow you to the hotel?"

Her head swiveled toward him as she fumbled with the door handle. "That's okay. I have the address...and my weapon."

"I didn't mean... I wasn't implying..." He ran a hand over his mouth. What had he been implying? Ever since he'd found those bones, something had felt off about the island. Some creeping menace had invaded the forest, the bay, the rivers and creeks. But he knew that menace had always been here.

She flashed her phone at him. "I'll follow the GPS. I'll be fine, but I wouldn't mind your cell phone number...just in case."

Had he ever *not* given his number to a pretty woman? Especially a knockout like Blanca Lopez. He was beginning to feel like his old self again.

"Sure, of course." He entered his number in her phone and when the call rang through to his phone, he saved her in his contacts.

As they got to his front door, he opened it and ushered her in ahead of him. "I'll get your suitcase from upstairs."

He bounded up the stairs and veered into the guest

room. He tripped to a stop as the scent of Blanca's perfume engulfed him—sweet with a hint of spice. He'd seen both sides of her already.

The sleek pantsuit she'd worn earlier sat at the edge of the bed in a neatly folded stack, her high heels on the floor, one shoe on its side. Her suitcase gaped open on the floor.

He opened his mouth to call her upstairs to pack away her clothes and then mentally shrugged. He wouldn't be handling any of her personal items by putting her suit and shoes on top of the other clothes in the bag.

He lifted the clothes and put them in the suitcase. Then he shoved her heels into the edges of the bag. As he reached for the lid to close the suitcase, he noticed an array of pastel-colored panties and lacy bras zipped into the top. He slammed the lid and zipped it.

Feeling like a perv, he wheeled the bag out of the room and hit the lights behind him. He grabbed the handle to carry it downstairs and almost tumbled to the bottom when he noticed Blanca, puffer jacket off, her arms inside her sweater as the empty sleeves dangled on either side of her body.

"Uh, excuse me?"

She looked up, her dark hair falling into her face as it came loose from her bun. "Oh, I'm just taking off your sister's thermal."

She turned her back on him and continued to wriggle inside the sweater. With a flourish, she pulled the white shirt from inside her sweater and dangled it in the air. "Ta-da!"

"Impressive." He did a slow clap.

She stuffed her arms into the sleeves and folded the thermal. "Thank you so much for this."

"You could've kept it. It's only going to get colder on the island."

"I'll do a little shopping while I'm here." She placed the shirt on the arm of a chair and patted it. "Tomorrow, then?"

He raised his eyebrows as he wheeled her suitcase to the door. "Tomorrow?"

"Mrs. Ruesler. I have her address, although I suppose you already know where she lives. I'll swing by and pick you up around ten o'clock, if that's okay."

"Right. Sure." He dragged her bag over the uneven surface of his driveway and listened for the pop of the trunk before nudging it open. He was hoping Blanca would've forgotten about asking him to accompany her to Birdie Ruesler's place. He'd rather sit on the edge of Dead Falls than return to that house, but he didn't want to give Blanca the wrong impression. Saying no would seem strange.

He hoisted her bag into the trunk, eyeing the boxes that contained Jeremy's case.

Blanca touched his arm. "Have you ever read the case files?"

"Nope." He slammed the trunk, and Blanca's hand fell from his arm.

"Would you like to?"

"Maybe." He stepped around her and opened the driver's-side door. "Drive carefully."

"Thanks." She slid behind the wheel and turned

her head toward him. "I'm sure the sheriff's department and Noah's parents were glad you were on the search tonight."

She still thought some subconscious memory had led him to that spot.

"I'm glad I was there, too. Good night, Blanca."

She swung her door shut and started the engine. He watched her car until the taillights disappeared over the first ridge. Then he headed back inside.

When he secured the house, he swept up his sister's thermal and pressed it to his face. The warmth of Blanca's body still clung to the light material, and the scent of her skin invaded his senses.

He didn't believe the answers to Jeremy's disappearance lay in his subconscious, but if Blanca Lopez thought so, he'd humor her just to explore this attraction between them.

BLANCA TOOK THE hotel clerk's recommendation and had breakfast at the café down the street. As she bit into a second piece of crisp bacon and savored the smoky flavor, she was glad she had.

She glanced at her phone. The Dead Falls Sheriff's Department had promised to keep her posted on the Noah Fielding case, but so far they didn't have the results of the DNA test on the hat. She had her own buccal swab kit in her briefcase, ready for Mrs. Ruesler.

Mrs. Ruesler had been notified about the discovery of the bones. Maybe she'd see the sense in giving her DNA now, especially as they didn't have Jeremy's anymore. DNA only worked for cold cases if it hadn't been corrupted.

Her phone buzzed on the table, and she lunged for it. She paused and caught her breath when she saw the number. She couldn't avoid him forever.

She tapped the display to answer. "Hello, Manny."

"There's my girl."

Her breakfast churned in her stomach. "I'm not your *girl*, Manny. What do you want?"

"That's what I admire about you, Blanca, always right to the point." He coughed. "Of course, that's not the only thing I admire about you."

"Get to it, Manny. I'm busy." She took a sip of water and swished it in her mouth.

He sucked in a sharp breath. "I heard you're out in the middle of nowhere investigating a cold case. Ouch."

"It's a missing boy. I'd say that's important."

"Yeah, but a nineteen-year-old cold case. One kid, not even a serial." He clucked his tongue. "You could've had it all, babe. You hear about the freeway shootings in Atlanta? That's my case."

"Congratulations, Manny. Is that what you called to tell me?"

"No. Hey, just wanted to let you know if you need any help or advice out there on that island, let me know. I'd be happy to lend my expertise. I've worked a couple of cold—"

Not needing nor wanting to hear another litany of his cases, she interrupted Manny. "Gotta go. Say hello to your wife for me."

She ended the call with a smile and stuffed the last forkful of eggs into her mouth. She had an appointment with a real man.

Getting close to Tate Mitchell would be invaluable for her. The way his blue eyes burned with intensity didn't hurt, either.

She left a hefty tip for the waitress and plugged in Tate's location again. She could probably get back there without directions, but a lot of these little roads off the main highway looked the same.

Twenty minutes later, she pulled behind his Jeep and honked the horn. He must've been waiting for her because he stepped out onto the porch immediately. He waved and turned to lock the door.

That gave her an opportunity to drink in his masculine form, the down vest he wore over a blue fleece Henley that had to match his eyes, enhancing his broad shoulders. She whistled softly between her teeth.

She powered down the window as he approached. "Is it okay if I drive? If not, we can switch cars."

"No, I prefer it. I can navigate." He circled the car and dropped into the passenger seat beside her.

He even smelled like the outdoors—in a good way—smoky, piney and fresh. He must bathe in it, or it was in his pores. That should've been her first clue about Manny. He smelled like expensive men's cologne, which he splashed on to hide his deceit.

"You ready?"

She started at the sound of his voice. "Yeah, I have the address in my phone."

"No need. I know how to get there. I'll guide you."
He jerked his thumb to the left. "Go toward the falls,
but you're not going to cross the bridge. Birdie—
Mrs. Ruesler lives on this side."

"Her name's Birdie?"

"Yeah, but I've always called her Mrs. Ruesler,
and Birdie doesn't fit her much anymore."

Blanca's bottom lip quivered. "I don't know how
anyone lives through the loss of a child, especially
one that age."

"If you wanna call it living." Tate slouched in his
seat and barked out the next set of directions.

She slid a glance at him. Had he gotten up on the
wrong side of the bed?

She cleared her throat. "I haven't heard from Deputy Cheswick yet about the beanie you found."

"He's in charge of the investigation? I thought he
was just in charge of the search parties last night."

"He's the one who told me he'd contact me. Where
was Sheriff Hopkins last night? I didn't see him.
Shouldn't he be in charge of a case like this?"

"You'll come to find out Sheriff Hopkins is lazy.
He likes the position, not the job."

"Yeah, I know a few people like that in the FBI."
She gripped the steering wheel and took the next
turn a little faster than she'd intended.

Minutes later, Tate directed her into a small subdivision of houses with neatly manicured lawns and
spiffy paint jobs. He pointed ahead. "Mrs. Ruesler's
house is on the left, second to the end."

Blanca's gaze tracked to the only house on the

block with an overgrown yard, a broken fence and paint peeling from the clapboard. She sucked in a breath. "Can't someone help her out?"

"I—I didn't realize she'd let the house go like this. Haven't been out this way for a while." Tate rubbed his eyes. "She's expecting you?"

"Not exactly." Blanca made a U-turn at the end of the block and pulled up to the curb in front of the neglected house. She opened her door and paused, as Tate seemed frozen in his seat. "You coming?"

"Right behind you."

Blanca's low-heeled boots scuffed against the leaves carpeting the walkway up to the porch. She took a big step over a piece of rotting wood and knocked on the door, glancing over her shoulder at Tate waiting at the bottom of the steps, his hands shoved in his pockets.

Shuffling noises answered Blanca's knock, and she felt, rather than saw, an eye peering at her from the peephole. "Mrs. Ruesler? I'm FBI Special Agent Blanca Lopez. I've been assigned to your son's cold case. Tate Mitchell is with me."

The door creaked open, and a woman with white, fluffy hair stared at her from the crack. "FBI? Is it about those bones?"

Blanca eased out a breath. At least she wouldn't be coming in cold here. "Yes, it is, Mrs. Ruesler. Can we come in?"

Mrs. Ruesler widened the door, her gaze traveling over Blanca's shoulder to take in Tate behind her. The woman's thin lips tightened, and her nostrils flared.

For a second, Blanca feared Mrs. Ruesler would

deny Tate entry to her home. She'd thought having Tate as her wingman would help her out, but the animosity pouring from Mrs. Ruesler threatened to bowl them both over.

Then Mrs. Ruesler backed up into the house and said, "Suit yourselves."

Blanca followed Mrs. Ruesler, and Tate came in behind her. He had to slam the warped door to get it to shut properly, and Blanca jumped. It didn't bother Mrs. Ruesler, though.

She turned to face Blanca, folding her scrawny arms over her sunken chest, covered in a baggy, checked blouse with the sleeves rolled up to her elbows. "What do you want?"

"Can we sit down?" Blanca gestured to the threadbare sofa as Tate stood awkwardly near the door, as if ready to give flight at any moment. He and Mrs. Ruesler hadn't exchanged one word.

"Go ahead." Mrs. Ruesler sank into the chair across from the sofa, her backside dropping into a well in the flattened cushion.

Blanca noticed that the chair Mrs. Ruesler had probably occupied for the past twenty years faced the front window. How long had she sat there waiting for Jeremy?

Placing the bag containing the DNA test kit at her feet, Blanca cleared her throat. "As you know, Mrs. Ruesler, a set of bones was discovered last week during a forest fire."

"By him." Mrs. Ruesler pointed a crooked finger at Tate, who stiffened beside Blanca on the sofa.

"That's right. I stumbled upon a set of bones. Forensics is ready to analyze them, but Agent Lopez told me the DNA they had from Jeremy has been corrupted. They don't have anything they can compare with the genetic material from the bones to find out if they belong to Jeremy."

Mrs. Ruesler's dull eyes shifted from Tate to Blanca. "Is that true?"

"Yes, unfortunately. These things can happen with cold cases."

"So you're here for my DNA. Is that right? You think my boy is dead and someone dumped his body in the forest." She looked past them through the window.

"If it's okay with you, we'd like to get a sample from you, Mrs. Ruesler." Blanca patted the bag on the floor. "We can do it right here. You don't need to come into the station. I'm trained to take the sample. It would…help to know, wouldn't it?"

Blanca held her breath, as the woman slowly dragged her gaze from the window and settled it on the bag. "I don't know if it would help."

"Listen, Birdie." Tate sat forward on the edge of the sofa, bracing his elbows on his knees. "If the FBI can positively identify Jeremy's…remains, Agent Lopez can start working on the case. Maybe we can find out who did this. Find out what happened."

Mrs. Ruesler ignored Tate and spoke directly to Blanca. "I'll let you take a sample. I know if I refuse, you'll just go to my daughter Celine in Boise and get it from her. She'd do it, but I don't want you bothering her. She has her own life—away from this place."

Blanca gave her a small smile. "It's the right decision. Can we sit at the kitchen table?"

Mrs. Ruesler nodded and made a move to rise from the chair. She struggled against the soft cushion, and Tate jumped up to take her arm. She put a clawlike hand on his forearm and then when she got to her feet dropped it as if it burned.

Blanca kept her face impassive at this exchange. Tate had seemed reluctant when she'd suggested he accompany her here, and now she knew why.

When she sat at the kitchen table with Mrs. Ruesler, Tate stood apart, looking out the kitchen window to the backyard. Blanca swabbed the inside of Mrs. Ruesler's mouth and bagged the swab, sealing it and dropping it into an envelope.

"That's it. We'll keep you posted."

Tate had already moved to the front door and hovered there as Blanca packed up the bag.

She said, "I promise you, Mrs. Ruesler. I'll do everything in my power to solve this case, even if those bones don't belong to Jeremy."

The older woman shoved her chair back so hard it hit the wall. "Everything? Then, ask him."

Tate closed his eyes as Jeremy's distraught mother jabbed a finger at him. "Ask him what he knows. Ask him why he came home to his parents and Jeremy didn't. Ask him about the Whistler."

Chapter Five

Tate could feel the blood drain from his face. He grabbed the door handle to steady himself, as his rubbery knees threatened to fail him.

The Whistler. How did she know about the Whistler?

He licked his lips. He wanted to turn and run out of the house, just as he and Jeremy used to when Mrs. Ruesler caught them stealing cookies tagged for the bake sale or when they'd let Jeremy's dog on the bed with them in her immaculate home. But he wasn't a kid anymore, and Birdie no longer treated him like a son. She hated him.

"Birdie." He reached out a hand but snatched it back when she screamed at him.

"It's your fault! It's your fault he's gone. He wanted to be just like you. He followed you. He did everything you told him to do." She clawed at her white hair. "What did you tell him to do that day? Why did you come home without him?"

Tate took a step forward, but Blanca shook her head at him and tipped her head at the door.

As he turned to leave, he saw Blanca take Birdie's arm and lead her back to the living room.

After he jogged through the broken gate, he paced outside Blanca's car along the sidewalk he'd once known as well as the one that fronted his parents' house. The cold air hit his hot cheeks, and he could almost hear the sizzle of contact.

He'd heard the whistle last night when he found the bloody cap. What was the tune? What did it mean, and how was it connected to Jeremy's disappearance?

Blanca exited the house and strode down the walkway. When she aimed the remote at the car, he circled around and opened the back door for her.

"I'll take that." He grabbed her bag with the precious DNA sample and put it on the seat. By the time he backed out of the car, Blanca was seated behind the wheel. He slid into the passenger seat.

"That went well." A muscle ticked in his jaw, and he pressed a thumb against it.

She took a deep breath. "Are you all right?"

Jerking his head to the side, he said, "Me? You should be asking if Mrs. Ruesler is all right."

"I know she's fine. I settled her down in her favorite chair and brought her a cup of tea. She'll be okay." She placed a hand on his arm. "Will you?"

With a creeping dread, Tate felt tears pricking behind his eyes. He was a grown man. He was not a twelve-year-old boy. He ran a hand beneath his nose. "I'm fine. I sort of expected that. I haven't seen Birdie for a while, but it always ends the same way, her blaming me for Jeremy's disappearance. I thought it might go differently this time—I mean, with the discovery of the bones and you being here."

"That must be hard for you to hear. Of course it wasn't your fault, Tate."

"Wasn't it?" He covered his eyes with his hand. He'd always gotten the girl by being carefree, happy-go-lucky, charming. He'd never tried crying before.

Blanca squeezed his shoulder. "Is that how you feel?"

"I suppose." It had been a long time since someone had offered him any sympathy. Most people had moved on. Even his sister didn't bring up Jeremy anymore. "It's survivor's guilt, isn't it? Someone took Jeremy that night and left me. Why? Why didn't he take both of us?"

"I think the most logical answer to that is there was only one perpetrator and two preteen boys. He couldn't handle both of you at the same time. Were you bigger, stronger than Jeremy?"

"Not really." He rubbed his chin. "We were about the same height. I was a skinny kid but always athletic. Jeremy still had some baby fat on him. I think he was getting ready for a growth spurt. His dad is tall, like really tall, and I think Jeremy was going to catch up to his old man."

"So Jeremy was slower than you?"

Tate caught a glimpse of shifting curtains at the window. "Can we get out of here?"

Blanca started the engine and pulled away from the Ruesler house. "Slower? Maybe that's why it was Jeremy instead of you."

"I don't know. We were on bikes. He could pedal just as fast as I could."

"But you didn't stay on the bikes, did you?" Blanca took a careful turn out of the subdivision. "That blood in your shoes was your own. Your socks were tattered, and your feet were bleeding. You lost your shoes at some point."

"I can't remember." He pinched the bridge of his nose.

Blanca remained silent as she navigated her way to the main highway. Then she gave a little cough. "What did Mrs. Ruesler mean about the Whistler? Who's the Whistler?"

Tate scooped a hand through his hair, digging his nails into his scalp. "I—I don't know. I don't know why she said that."

"Yeah, you do." Blanca glanced at him with narrowed eyes. "The look on your face when she mentioned the Whistler said it all."

Tate's head snapped back. What happened to the comforting words? "It did?"

Tapping her fingers on the steering wheel, she said, "I don't recall anything about a Whistler in the summary I read, but I haven't gotten to the file notes yet. Will I find anything there?"

"I told you. I never read them."

"Something about her words triggered you. What was it?" She smacked the dashboard with her hand. "C'mon, Tate. This isn't a date where you're trying to impress the girl. If I have any hope of solving this case, I'm going to need the only witness to Jeremy's disappearance to come clean with me. What do you know about the Whistler?"

Tate squeezed his eyes closed and willed himself back in the forest when he found Noah's beanie. He'd heard whistling then—in his head. Why? How had Birdie known about it?

"Okay." He gripped his knees and hunched forward. "Last night when I found Noah's cap, I lost it for a few minutes. Felt disconnected from my body. I heard…whistling."

"Whistling? Like wind whistling through the trees or a human whistling?"

"Human. Someone whistling a tune." He whipped his head around. "How did Mrs. Ruesler know that I heard something last night? I must've said something about whistling at the time of Jeremy's disappearance, but I don't remember now."

"Do you remember the tune?"

"I don't." He rolled his eyes upward, as if he could find the answer on the ceiling of the car. "It was maybe a kids' song or something like that. I mean, that's what I heard last night."

"Could you duplicate it now?" She lifted her eyebrows. "If you whistle it, maybe I could recognize it."

"Do you have kids?" He eyed her left hand on the steering wheel, devoid of jewelry. Lots of married women didn't wear wedding ring, so he'd try the direct approach here.

"I don't have kids, but I have several siblings with kids, and when I'm in LA, Auntie Blanca is the go-to babysitter. I've watched my fair share of cartoons."

She nudged his arm with her elbow. "So go ahead, put your lips together and blow."

He watched her pucker her own plump lips and decided she couldn't possibly be married, not the way she was flirting with him.

Spreading his hands, he said, "I wouldn't know where to start. I can't remember the tune—last night or before. I just know it wasn't random whistling."

"Then, we have a date tonight."

"We do?"

"I haven't had a minute to dig into the files yet, and you've never looked at them at all. Sounds like we have some work ahead of us."

From sympathetic cop to hard-hitting interrogator to flirtatious siren, this woman gave him whiplash. "Where does the date part come in?"

"I will order pizza and buy a six-pack for sustenance before we dig into the files in my hotel room. Deal?"

"Only if we order from Luigi's and you let me pick it up on the way."

"Does Luigi's deliver to my hotel?"

"I'm sure they do, but it's on my way."

"Tell you what." She swung into his driveway, the gravel and dirt crunching beneath the tires. "I'll spring for the pizza because the agency will pay for food. You grab the beer, which doesn't fall into my reimbursement category."

"What time?"

"Let's make it seven o'clock." She leveled a finger at him, as he got out of the car. "But don't for one second think just because we're eating pizza and throwing back a few beers that I'm gonna go easy on you, Tate."

He saluted and said, "Yes, ma'am," before slamming the car door and stepping back.

As she drove away with a wave out the window, he whispered. "Oh, please, please don't go easy on me."

AFTER SENDING MRS. RUESLER'S DNA sample to the FBI lab, Blanca spent the rest of the day with the Dead Falls sheriff's deputies on the Noah Fielding case. She met Mr. and Mrs. Fielding and saw the same lost look she'd seen in Mrs. Ruesler's eyes. Only, Mrs. Ruesler's had hardened into hopelessness. She'd do everything in her power to keep that from happening to the Fieldings.

She'd grabbed a quick sandwich for lunch while poring over the pithy witness statements they'd received on Noah's case. A few people had seen him leave the campsite, and a few more noticed him walking along the river, but nobody reported seeing anyone else in his vicinity—and nobody mentioned any whistling.

Her stomach rumbled as she packed it in for the day, so when she noticed Luigi's Pizza on her way back to her hotel, she pulled into the parking lot. As she sat in her car, she called Tate.

He picked up after the first ring. "Are we still on?"

"I'm sitting in front of Luigi's as we speak. Just wanted to check if you're a kitchen-sink guy, a minimalist or a weird pineapple type."

"Kitchen sink." He cleared his throat. "And are you a standard Bud girl, foreign imports or craft beer?"

"All of the above. Surprise me."

She couldn't wipe the smile from her face as she practically skipped into Luigi's. She hadn't been on a date since that fiasco with Manny—not that this was a date. Pizza, beer and work did not equal a date.

The warmth of the restaurant engulfed her when she walked in, the smell of garlic and oregano permeating the air. Few empty tables verified Tate's assertion that Luigi's ruled. Blanca joined the line for takeout orders, her head tilted back as she studied the menu above the counter.

When she reached the front, she ordered an extra-large supreme and a Diet Coke. After paying with her government credit card, she skirted the counter, paper cup in hand and joined another line for the soda machine.

She filled her cup with ice and soda, snapped on a lid, grabbed a straw and headed for the wooden bench that lined the wall in the front of the restaurant. Perching on the edge of the bench, she sucked down the icy drink.

A man sat heavily beside her, holding his own drink, his shoulder jostling hers. She scooted to the side to create some separation.

The man turned his head. "I'm sorry. Am I crowding you?"

"It's a crowded place." She uncrossed her legs and put her knees together.

His eyes popped open. "I know you. You're the FBI

agent the sheriff's brought in for the Jeremy Ruesler case."

Her gaze darted among the people waiting for their food, but although the man's voice sounded like a shout to her, nobody seemed to notice.

Dipping her head, she said, "That's right."

"Terrible business. And the new case? This tourist boy? Do you think it's related? Kind of suspicious Tate finds those bones and another boy goes missing." He shook his finger. "There have been others, too, but nobody wants to talk about those."

"Others?" He had her full attention now. "Other missing boys here on Dead Falls?"

"Let's just say Dead Falls isn't the only island in Discovery Bay." He jumped to his feet. "That's me."

"Wait." She stood up beside him and grabbed his jacket. "Who are these other boys? Can you give me a name?"

He squinted, the light freckles on his face bunching around his nose. "Andrew. Andrew Finnigan for starters."

She typed the name into her phone, as the red-haired stranger grabbed a stack of pizzas and barreled out of the restaurant without giving her any more names.

Was this guy serious, or was he just trying to insert himself into the case? How had he recognized her? Had to be a serious follower of the case to know her identity.

When she heard her number, she scurried to the soda machine for a refill before picking up the gigantic pizza and balancing her cup on top of the box, a plastic bag with paper plates, napkins and utensils swinging from her wrist. A kind soul opened the door for her, and she whisked the pizza back to the car and put it on the front seat.

By the time she got to her hotel, she had about twenty minutes to make herself decent. She slid the pizza box onto the credenza next to the microwave and hit the shower.

She'd scaled down her work clothes today, ditching the high heels for a pair of low-heeled boots and replacing the blouse and jacket with a sweater, but she still couldn't bring herself to adopt jeans for work attire, even out here in the wilderness, and that didn't have to mark her as Manny's protege. She'd been forging her own work style lately, forcing Manny's voice from her head.

She took a quick shower, releasing her hair from its ponytail and scrunching up her waves with wet hands. She slipped into a pair of jeans and ducked into a fresh sweater. She checked her pedicure before leaving her feet bare and spritzed on a little perfume.

The knock on the door came before she could freshen her makeup. She checked herself in the full-length mirror before opening the door.

Tate held up two six-packs of bottled beer—a mixture of IPAs in one and a Mexican beer in the other.

"Ooh, you're my new best friend." She took the pack of IPAs from his hand. "And they're cold."

Lifting his nose in the air, he sniffed. "And you're mine. How was Luigi's?"

"Crowded…and weird." She plucked a bottle from the carrier and held it up. As he nodded, she used an opener from the hotel to snap off the lid.

"Weird how?" He thanked her for the beer and took a gulp.

"Some guy there recognized me and asked me about the cases. Said there were other missing boys in Discovery Bay that the sheriffs haven't looked at."

"He might be talking about a few runaways. A few accidental deaths."

"Andrew Finnigan ring any bells?"

"Yeah, one of the accidentals." He tapped the box. "I'm starving."

"Do you want me to put a couple of slices in the microwave? I picked it up over a half hour ago."

"I don't like what the microwave does to the crust. I'm good. You?"

"Lukewarm pizza is fine by me." She opened the plastic bag from Luigi's and peeled off a couple paper plates from the stack they'd given her. She placed them on the credenza and dropped some napkins beside them.

Tate had flipped open the pizza box, and the aroma of Italian spices filled the hotel room. He nudged the box toward her. "You first."

Blanca used her fingers and a plastic knife to separate a large piece of pizza from the whole and plopped it onto her plate. A clump of cheese stuck to the knife, and she licked it off. Then she lowered herself to the sofa, placing her plate on the coffee table in front of it.

Kicking a box on the floor, she said, "I have the files right here. Sustenance first and then we'll do a deep dive…into the case."

Tate settled next to her. "I think I'm going to need a lot of sustenance to get through those boxes."

"I can't believe you never looked through the files before." She took a dainty sip of beer before tearing into her first piece of pizza.

"Nobody ever offered when I was an adult. I just didn't think it was worth it." He tapped his bottle with his finger. "You like the beer? It's from a microbrewery in Seattle."

She smacked her lips. "It's citrusy and piney all at once. It tastes like this island."

Tasted like she imagined Tate would taste. She stuffed more pizza in her mouth before she blurted out something inappropriate.

"And the pizza?"

With her mouth full, she gave him a thumbs-up sign.

They scarfed down more than half the pizza and drank two beers each before Blanca pushed up from the sofa and made a beeline toward the bathroom. "I'm going to wash my hands first. I don't want to leave pizza grease on the files."

"Good point. Jeremy's DNA was already disqualified. We don't need to add any more corruption."

Blanca turned from the sink with her hands dripping and ran into Tate, hovering behind her. The small space practically smooshed her nose into his chest. "Sorry. Just grabbing a towel."

Tate whipped it off the rack and handed it to her.

She took it from him and stepped to the side to dry her hands, as he slid into her place at the sink. She wanted to use it to cover her heated cheeks instead.

She hung the towel back on the rack when she finished and then hurried back to the other room, fanning herself. If she planned to work with this guy closely, she'd better get a grip. She didn't need to get caught in the trap of falling for every man she worked with. Her rep had already taken a hit once.

She cleared the plates from the coffee table, leaving their beers, and scooped out a handful of file folders from the first box. She plopped them on the table just as Tate joined her. "Here we go."

"What are we gonna start with here?" He downed the dregs of his beer, as if he needed the liquid courage to continue.

Tapping the file on top, she said, "These are the witness statements, including your own, which the deputies conducted in the hospital. Do you remember that?"

"I remember." His blue eyes stared past her shoulder, their glassiness giving them an otherworldly appearance. Was he seeing into the past now? Would that help him recall what happened that night?

Blanca scooted close to him, until her thigh pressed against his, and slipped open the folder on the table, so they could both see the contents. She ran the tip of her finger down a short list of names. "These are the people who were in the general area that night, or I guess late afternoon. That's when it happened, right? Late afternoon? They found you at night, but that's not when Jeremy disappeared. You'd mentioned something about your parents not allowing you in the forest at night."

"Did I?" He tugged on an earlobe, the gesture seeming to bring him back to the present. "That's right. No way our parents would've allowed us out after dark, but it was summertime and the sun set late. We left Jeremy's house around three o'clock in the afternoon that day."

She shuffled through some papers. "They found you at eleven o'clock at night. You were tied to a tree, and you had a contusion on your head." She peered at a form from the hospital. "The doc thinks that's why you couldn't remember anything."

"Probably." Tate rubbed the back of his head, as if touching the phantom wound. "But how would the kidnapper know that? He couldn't have known that a blow to the back of my head would cause amnesia."

"What's your point?" She peered at him over the top of the paper.

"After the abduction, my parents were terrified that the man would come for me to shut me up…but he never did. He wasn't worried that I'd be able to identify him because I probably never saw him." He shifted on the sofa, and Blanca tipped toward him, bumping his shoulder with hers. "Look, Jeremy and I didn't always ride bikes side by side. We'd take different paths sometimes. He was on the wrong path at the wrong time, and someone took him. The kidnapper realized too late that Jeremy wasn't alone, so he hit me on the head and tied me up to that tree to give him some time to get away with Jeremy. I never saw him, and he knew that. I was no threat to him. I'm still not a threat to him."

"But you heard a whistle."

Tate lifted the box by the corner and dropped it. "Is that in there? Nobody ever asked me about whistling before…before Mrs. Ruesler brought it up."

"You heard it last night when you found Noah's cap. You heard it *before* we talked to Mrs. Ruesler." Blanca plunged her hands in the box. "You must've told somebody."

Tate eyed the pages she'd fanned out on the table. Blanca picked out all the pieces of paper that contained witness statements and interviews. "If I could get the online files, we could just do a search for whistling, but we'll have to sift through the old-fashioned way. You take half, and I'll take half."

Sliding half the pages to his side of the table, Tate said, "We can try."

They worked in silence for several minutes, or almost silence. Tate would catch his breath or sigh or click his tongue as he shuffled through the pages.

As Blanca stood up to stretch, he jabbed a piece of paper with his finger. "Here it is."

Blanca stopped midstretch and plopped on the sofa next to him. "You found something?"

He picked up the page and waved it in the air. "It's an interview with Birdie. She said I'd told her someone had been whistling in the forest while Jeremy and I were playing. That we kept hearing it, and then it would go away."

Blanca sucked in her bottom lip. "She said you said. Secondhand. Did you ever tell the police that? Did they ever follow up with any of the other witnesses?"

"Not that I've come across yet. I don't even remember telling her that."

"What was the tune?" She snatched the paper from his hand.

Instead of an answer, Tate began to whistle the "Hokey Pokey" song, but instead of the upbeat melody designed to get you to put your various body parts in and out, he'd slowed it down so it sounded like a creepy warning.

"Really? The 'Hokey Pokey' song? We played that when we were kids." Her gaze raked the questions and answers with Mrs. Ruesler, and a chill touched the back of her neck when she read her words.

She held out the paper with an unsteady hand. "Mrs. Ruesler doesn't name the tune here, Tate. She said you told her you didn't know what it was and couldn't repeat it."

Tate lifted his icy blue gaze to her face. "I know. I just remembered it."

Chapter Six

Tate sprang to his feet and jerked open the door to the mini fridge. He grabbed a bottle of beer and pried the cap off on the edge of the credenza. He practically poured the alcohol down his throat to drown the feeling of dread gathering in his gut.

How come he'd never remembered that tune before? How many times had he heard that song when his nephew had been a toddler? How many times had it brought him no other emotion except annoyance?

He glanced at Blanca who had her arms crossed over her chest. "You're kidding. You just remembered the song now?"

"It's the tune I heard in my head last night. It hit me right here." He pounded his chest with his fist. "Like a sledgehammer."

"You heard him whistle it like that? Slow? It's usually kind of fast and chirpy."

"I have no idea. What did Birdie say?" He took a long step over the coffee table and snatched up the piece of paper Blanca had dropped on the floor. He skimmed the words until he found the spot. *"Tate told me he didn't see anyone while the boys were playing, but he and Jeremy heard someone whistling a tune. He didn't know what song it was. They heard it more than once and in different locations in the forest. They thought someone was following them. They thought it was a joke."*

"Wow." Blanca rose to her feet and paced the length of the room. "Why do you think you didn't tell the police the same thing?"

"Not sure." Tate finished off the first beer and grabbed another, taking a long slug. "All I remember about that interrogation is people seemed to think it was my fault. My idea to go riding. My idea to go deep into the forest. My idea to stay out late. That I was saying and doing whatever I thought might get me off the hook. Maybe I thought if I'd told the deputies about the whistling, they'd get mad at me for not telling them before, or they'd tell me I should've known we were being followed. Or maybe I just told Mrs. Ruesler about a whistler because I thought she needed to hear something—anything."

"You don't believe that. You remembered the whistling before she said anything about it. The rest…" Her dark eyes shimmered as she walked toward him. She circled the coffee table and placed both hands on his shoulders. "I'm sorry they made you feel that way. They should've had a therapist talk to you."

"That's what my buddy's fiancée does. She's a forensic psychologist who specializes in children. Maybe if I'd had someone like Hannah Maddox on my side all those years ago, I would've been able to help the sheriff's department solve the case."

She squeezed his shoulders. "You were a kid. It wasn't up to you to solve the case."

"But you think it is now?" He narrowed his eyes.

Blanca dropped her hands and took a step back. "You're not a kid anymore. Maybe something can jog your memory—it just did. Thinking about the whistling that night prompted you to remember the tune."

He downed the rest of his second beer and swiped a hand across his mouth. "Now if we can just interrogate every man on the island who whistles."

"It's a start. Not many men wander around whistling the 'Hokey Pokey' tune."

Tate held up his empty bottle. "I'm going for another. Do you want the remaining IPA? I'll take the other."

Raising her eyebrows, she asked, "Are you going to be able to drive? That'll be your third."

"Two and then one more after a break and several slices of pizza?" He stopped and covered his heart with his hand. "That's what all drunk drivers say, isn't it?"

"I—I'm not implying that you're drunk."

"I know, but you're right." He walked to the recycling trash and dropped his bottle into it. "If I had another, I'd have to spend the night."

Blanca's dark eyes brightened as a rosy pink touched her cheeks. "If that's what you want, go for it. The sofa pulls out to a bed."

"I'm good." He held up his hands. "I think I've had enough tonight."

"Enough beer or enough memories?"

"Maybe both." He gathered up the rest of their trash, stuffed it in the plastic bag from Luigi's and shoved it into the small waste basket.

She perched on the edge of the sofa. "I think it's a good clue, Tate. If any of the people who were near the site of Noah's abduction heard whistling, that could link the two cases."

"Do you really think the person who kidnapped Jeremy almost twenty years ago is active again? Why? How?"

Blanca held up her hand and ticked off her fingers. "You find bones. Boy is same age. Same MO. You found his cap."

"Didn't you learn at the academy that the chances of a kidnapper, or any kind of criminal, staying dormant for twenty years is atypical?" He jabbed his thumb into his chest. "Even I know that."

"Was he really dormant? You said it yourself. Boys have gone missing from the island in the interim. What if those weren't runaways or accidents?" She snapped her fingers. "That guy at the pizza place mentioned that other islands in Discovery Bay may have had similar cases."

"I didn't pay that much attention. If the Dead Falls Sheriff's Department called the boys missing or runaways, I figured they had a reason, and the other islands in the bay are small. Dead Falls is the biggest."

"You told me yourself the sheriff's department is incompetent. How long have they been inept?"

"Wait a minute." He shook his head. "I didn't mean every deputy in the department. We have some good people. It's the current sheriff, Hopkins, and the one before him, my friend Hannah's father, Sheriff Maddox—he was more corrupt than incompetent."

"Great. If they've been running things for a while, they could've missed signs. Even I can see Hopkins is lazy. It's a lot easier to call a twelve-year-old boy a runaway than actually launch an investigation, bring in the FBI."

Tate chewed on his bottom lip. "Are you going to look into some of those cases?"

"I am." She folded her arms as if she expected an argument from him, but who was he to disagree with the FBI?

If he stayed another minute, he'd need another beer. And if he had another beer, he'd have to stay in her hotel room. And if he stayed in her hotel room…

He coughed. "I gotta go. Thanks for the pizza."

She hopped off the arm of the sofa and tapped the pizza box. "Please take this with you when you leave, or I'll be tempted to sneak out here for a midnight snack."

"You have a fridge. Put a few slices in there and have it for breakfast." Tate reached for his hoodie.

"You're assuming I have any self-control at all." One dark eyebrow arched. "I don't."

And neither did he—not where Blanca Lopez was concerned.

"I'll do you this favor." He grabbed the pizza box. "But then you owe me."

"I'll let you know as soon as I hear anything about a DNA match between Mrs. Ruesler and the bones, and I'll let you know about the results of the blood on Noah's hat." She made a cross over her heart with her finger.

With an effort, he pulled his gaze away from the gesture. "That's no fun."

"Wh-what isn't?" She tilted her head, and her wavy dark hair cascaded over her shoulder.

"I'm not going to ask you for something you already want to give me." He winked and got the hell out her hotel room before he got in any deeper.

WHEN THE HOTEL door slammed behind Tate, Blanca exhaled and collapsed on the sofa. If he'd spent the night in her hotel room, she wouldn't have needed that pizza for a midnight snack. Groaning, she touched her forehead to her knees. What was with her? Did she give off some kind of flirty vibes with the men she worked with? She knew damned well she wasn't irresistible.

She gathered up the papers strewn across the coffee table and sorted them back into order. This plan had worked, even if Tate thought the information was worthless. A man who whistled a usually happy tune while he was stalking two boys gave off strong psycho vibes. How did someone like that hide in plain sight?

She finished packing the papers and then shifted

the box from the table to the floor, next to the other box. She flipped the lid off the second box and lifted a file folder filled with photos. She'd started their search with the other box for a reason. Better to ease Tate back into the case than slam him over the head with it.

She pinched the first photo between her thumb and index finger and studied the bloody shoes that had been on Tate's feet when the search team had found him. Nobody could figure out why the bottoms of Tate's feet were bloody when he had his shoes on. When had he taken them off? Had he lost them in his flight from the threat? Had the kidnapper then put Tate's shoes back on his feet when he'd tied him to that tree? Why? To reduce the amount of evidence at the scene?

Tate had been right about one thing. If he'd seen his friend's abductor, that monster never would've let him live. Even if Tate hadn't laid eyes on the man, why had he spared Tate's life? Put his shoes back on?

She picked up the next picture. The vacant stare from Tate's twelve-year-old self unnerved her. He'd been in shock. Scratches marred his face, where the hint of his strong jaw was just emerging from his chubby cheeks. A line of dried blood connected one of his nostrils to his top lip. The white edges of a bandage poked out behind his ear.

She traced a finger from the top of his messy blond hair to his chin and whispered, "What happened out there, Tate?"

Her phone buzzed, and she jumped. Had Tate remembered something else? She answered the call and said, "Did you have second thoughts about that pizza?"

A long pause on the other end sent her pulse into a flutter, and she glanced at the display, which she should've done in the first place.

Manny's voice purred in her ear. "Sharing pizza with someone at this time of night already, Blanca?"

Closing her eyes, she gripped the phone. "What do you want, Manny? If you don't stop calling and harassing me, I'm going to report you."

He clicked his tongue. "After what happened last time, nobody is going to believe you, sweetheart."

Shame burned her cheeks, and anger gave an edge to her tongue. She clamped her mouth shut before she showed him how much he still got to her. "What is it?"

"Wondering if you needed a little help with that cold case of yours, but it sounds like you may have found a source already to…work with. If you're eating pizza in your hotel room with him, you must be on the right track."

"How do you know it's a him, and how do you know I'm in my hotel room?" She scooted off the sofa and sauntered to the sliding glass doors to the small balcony. Twitching back the drapes, she stared at her reflection. Her balcony faced the hotel parking lot and a line of trees beyond—always trees hemming you in on this island. She yanked the drapes closed.

"Don't forget, B. I know you very well. *Very* well."

"I don't need your help, Manny, not now, not in

the future—never. All that time you pretended to help me, and you were just helping yourself. Now you can't stand it that I might find success, standing on my own two feet, proving you wrong. Back off. Don't call me again, or I will report you. And I don't give a damn what the agency thinks about it." She ended the call with a stab of her thumb and tossed the phone onto the sofa.

She placed the rest of the photos in the box and slid the lid back on it. Then she changed into a pair of flannel pajama bottoms and a camisole and washed her face. She grabbed her toothbrush and then set it on the edge of the sink.

Tate had left her one IPA, and she needed it. She padded into the sitting room and snagged the beer from the fridge. Aiming the remote at the TV, she dropped onto the bed and adjusted the pillows behind her. After a few sips of beer and ten minutes of a reality TV show, she set her bottle on the nightstand and wriggled off the bed.

She needed a snack with the beer. That pizza would've been better than a bag of chips, but she had to pretend to Tate that she was the kind of girl who didn't like to nosh into the night, diets be damned.

She opened her purse and slipped her debit card from her wallet. She had it on good authority that the vending machines on the fourth floor took plastic.

Clutching her debit card and her room key card, she crept down the hallway on bare feet to the elevator. A door behind her closed softly, but she didn't bother to turn around. When she entered the elevator, she pressed the button for the fourth floor, hoping she wouldn't run into any other late-night snackers.

The doors opened on an empty hallway, and she followed the low buzz of the ice machine. She hung a left across from the stairwell and stole into the room that housed an ice machine, soda machine and a tempting array of chips, cookies and candy.

Balancing one foot on top of the other, she studied the display in the case. Chips with her beer would be the natural choice, but that pizza had sated her salty craving. She needed something sweet.

She inserted her card, tapped the letter-number combo for a pack of cupcakes and bent down to retrieve them. A squeak of a shoe and a rustle behind her made her jerk her head up quickly.

Out of the corner of her eye, she saw an object flying toward her. It landed on the back of her head, and she opened her mouth to protest through her dizziness.

A hand clamped over her lips, a cloth pressing against her nose. She dragged in a breath and knew her mistake instantly, as a sweet smell invaded her nostrils and hit the back of her throat.

She dropped to the floor on her knees and saw her cupcakes in the dispenser as she keeled over.

Chapter Seven

Tate finished the last piece of pizza in his Jeep looking out at the falls—the falls where Andrew Finnigan's body had been found. He remembered the case. Andrew had gone missing after school one day. The boy had been a loner, troubled, drugs already at the age of thirteen.

Even his parents, who'd reported him missing at ten o'clock that night, had been more worried about suicide or running away than foul play. About a week later, his broken body had been discovered on the first ledge beneath the falls, and the sheriff's department had quickly ruled it an accidental death, a fall.

Some suspected suicide, but maybe the deputies were trying to spare Andrew's parents. In their haste to settle on a manner and cause of death, had law enforcement missed something? Andrew's death had occurred in the early 2000s. Tate had been away at college in Seattle during that time, but his sister had told him about it.

Tate had then read about the case and had been surprised that Andrew's body had remained intact for almost a week. Plenty of wild animals in the area could've made short work of his corpse. Sheriff Maddox was still very popular around that time. Had he wrapped up the investigation early to stoke that popularity? As corrupt as the man was, he was a lot more efficient than Hopkins.

Tate wiped his hands on a crumpled napkin and grabbed his phone. If Blanca planned to keep him updated on her side of the investigation, he owed it to her to feed her everything he remembered. She'd asked about Andrew before, and this information might give her a starting point.

He called her number, putting the phone on Speaker. It rang several times before going to voice mail. Tate ended the call and tried again. He sucked in his bottom lip. He'd heard her phone ring, and she had it on full blast. Would be hard for her to sleep through that, and that's why she had it that way. She didn't want to miss a thing.

She'd also mentioned that she was a night owl, and it wasn't even midnight yet. He tapped her contact info again. Maybe the beers had made her sleepy, although she'd seemed wired when he left her.

When he heard her voice mail pick up for a third time, he ended the call and dropped the phone on the console. She could wait until tomorrow for this information on Andrew. It wasn't going anywhere, but when he pulled away from the viewing point for the falls, he turned back toward town and her hotel instead of in the direction of his place.

A pulse throbbed at the base of his throat, and

his foot pressed the accelerator. He eased off the gas pedal when he hit the main road. She was probably sleeping. She didn't have to be at his beck and call. What excuse could he possibly give for showing up at her hotel room after he'd just left?

She'd laugh in his face if he told her the uneasiness he'd been feeling ever since he remembered that tune had filtered into his thoughts of her. A kidnapper of adolescent boys didn't pose any threat to Blanca—or to him, anymore.

Still, he drove straight back to her hotel and parked in the lot. She had a room on the second floor, and it faced the parking lot, but he couldn't tell from here which one she occupied. Lights glowed in only one window on the second floor, though, and the room, halfway down the hallway, could definitely be hers. So if she were awake with the lights on, why didn't she answer her phone?

With his pulse thrumming, Tate exited his car and strode toward the hotel entrance. He waved at the clerk, who'd been working earlier, and jogged to the stairwell. He took the stairs two at a time to the second floor and burst onto the hallway from the fire door.

He took a few deep breaths to control his panting and squared himself in front of Blanca's door. He tapped lightly, his ear to the door. When she didn't respond, he knocked louder and called her name.

"Blanca, I just thought of something." He could explain later that she hadn't answered her phone. He'd have a harder time explaining why this piece

of information about Andrew couldn't wait for tomorrow.

He rested his forehead against the door, pressing
his palms flat against it. "Blanca?"

Could she be sleeping? Her room was a suite with
a separate bedroom. She could have that door closed
and be dead to the world. A shiver ran up his spine.
He pulled out his phone and called her.

Holding his breath, he cocked his head toward
the door and heard the faint sound of her cell phone
ringing from the interior of the room. He took a step
back from the door so she would be able to see him
through the peephole…but only silence came from
the other side.

A door opened behind him, and he jumped.

A middle-aged woman, clutching a robe to her
throat with one hand, a half-full wineglass in the
other, peered at him. "Is that your room?"

"Uh, no. It's my friend's room. I was here earlier, and I…uh, forgot something. Sorry to disturb
you." He gestured toward Blanca's room. "She's either sound asleep, or she went out."

He doubted Blanca had left her room without her
phone.

"Oh, she went out." The woman swirled her wine,
seeming to enjoy her late-night encounter. "But that
was a while ago. I thought I heard her come back,
though."

"She went out?" Tate took a step toward the woman.
"You saw her go out?"

"Yeah." She aimed a toe at a tray on the floor.

"I was putting my room service out, and I saw her walking toward the elevator. I don't think she was planning to leave the hotel, though."

"How do you know that?"

"She was wearing what could've been pajamas, and she was barefoot. You wouldn't go outside like that, would you?" She took a sip of her wine and then waved the glass in the air unsteadily. "If you ask me, she was heading for the vending machines. I could've told her the hotel room service would deliver French fries…and even a bottle of wine."

"Vending machines? When was this? Wouldn't she be back by now?" Tate licked his dry lips. None of this made sense.

"Less than an hour ago, but probably more than thirty minutes. Maybe she got a snack and then took a midnight dip in the indoor pool." She flung her arm out. "You sure she's not in there? I could've sworn I heard a door open on the corridor."

"I don't think so." Tate eyed his phone. "Is the vending machine down the hallway toward the elevator?"

"Not on this floor. You have to go to the lobby or the fourth floor for the vending machines. I doubt she was going down to the lobby dressed like she was."

"Okay, thanks. I'll try the vending machines first."

As he marched back to the stairwell, the nosy neighbor called out. "And then try the pool, handsome. I wouldn't mind a little midnight skinny-dipping myself."

That woman didn't belong anywhere near water

right now. He climbed two flights of stairs to the fourth floor. Even if Blanca had gone to the vending machines, why would she still be there? Maybe she came back to her room and then left again. Maybe that's the door the guest heard. If she weren't there, if he couldn't find her, did he have a right to ask the hotel clerk to open her door?

What if she were in her room with someone? God, he'd never be able to face her again.

He cranked down the handle of the fire door to the fourth floor and bumped it open with his hip. The hum of the ice machine drew him toward an alcove a few doors down.

He drew up to the open door, and his heart slammed against his rib cage. "Blanca!"

He crouched beside her still form, her body on its side, one arm over her head, one flung across her chest. Thank God her chest rose and fell and her flesh was warm to his touch.

As he brought his face close to her mouth to check her breathing, a sickeningly sweet scent made him gag. He'd eaten a lot of those cupcakes sitting in that vending machine tray and none ever smelled like that.

Brushing a lock of her hair from her face, he said, "Blanca? Blanca, wake up."

She moaned softly from her parted lips.

Tate sprang up and got a bottle of water from the machine. He twisted off the cap and scooped an arm beneath Blanca to raise her to a sitting position between his legs, her back against his chest. He put the water to her lips and tipped a little of the liquid into her mouth.

"Drink this, Blanca. C'mon, wake up. You're okay." Actually, he wasn't sure if she was okay or not. He patted her head but didn't feel any bumps or sticky hair. He smoothed his hands down her bare arms and encircled her waist with his hands. No blood. No injuries.

Just the smell of ether emanating from the lower half of her face. Had someone done this to her? He knew people took strange things for a high, but he doubted an adult woman of means would use ether for a bump.

The water he poured into her mouth trickled down her chin, but she gurgled. He tried a little more and dabbed his wet fingers on her forehead. "Open your eyes, Blanca."

Her long dark lashes fluttered against her cheeks, and she began to slouch against his body. He wrapped an arm around her waist and hoisted her up, holding her against him.

"Drink the water." He tilted the bottle into her mouth, and she swallowed, even though more ran down her neck, soaking her cami top.

"Okay, we're gonna stand up. The sooner you get out of this lethargic state, the better." He maneuvered himself back into a crouch and hooked his arms beneath hers. He braced himself against the soda machine and straightened up, dragging her with him.

She wobbled and fell against his body.

"It's okay. I've got you. Just move one foot in front of the other."

She shuffled forward and then bent over at the waist, retching.

Patting her back, he said, "Attagirl. We can always clean up regurgitated pizza later."

Luckily, Blanca didn't throw up any pizza, but she had a few more dry heaves before uncurling her body. She listed to the side, and he caught her, planting one hand firmly on her hip.

"Let's go, sailor. Keep walking." As he watched her feet take a few more unsteady steps forward, Tate spotted a red credit card on the floor. With one hand tucked into the waistband of her flannel pajama bottoms, he ducked quickly to peel the card from the floor.

Blanca must've used it for the vending machines. His head swiveled as he searched the floor for any other items she might've had. His heart stuttered. Where was her room key?

Clamping Blanca's body next to his, Tate staggered down the hallway to the elevators. When they got to the lobby, he half dragged, half carried Blanca across the tiled floor to the reception desk.

The clerk's eyes widened at their approach. "Is Ms. Lopez okay? What happened?"

"I'm not sure yet—" Tate peered at the kid's name tag "—Richard, but she was by the vending machines, and she doesn't have her room key. Can you give me a card key for her room? I'll take her up and try to find out what happened."

"Sh-should I call the police?" Richard swallowed hard, his Adam's apple bobbing in his skinny neck dotted with acne.

"Not yet." Tate readjusted his hold on Blanca, fixing her top to cover her cleavage from Richard's goggling.

He didn't want the police involved yet—didn't want to get Blanca into any trouble, just in case. He really didn't know her. She could be hiding all kinds of secrets.

"Maybe you could look at the camera footage from the second and fourth floors, though, for any unusual activity."

"Sure, sure." Richard swiped a plastic card through a machine and handed it to Tate. "There you go. Room 226."

"Thanks, Richard. I'll let you know if we need to bring law enforcement into this."

Richard reached beneath the counter and shoved two bottles of water at Tate. "She might need these."

Having left the other bottle of water at the vending machine, Tate nodded, swiping up the bottles and holding them both in one hand as he navigated Blanca toward the elevator. "That's it. Keep walking. You're doing great."

When they got into the elevator car, Blanca leaned against the mirrored wall and wiped a hand across her mouth. At least she'd stopped gagging and heaving.

"How do you feel? You coming out of it?" He cracked open one of the water bottles and held it to her lips. "I think it was just chloroform. You're not gonna die."

She nodded, or maybe her chin just dropped to

her chest, but when she lifted her head, she drank some of the water without spewing it down her chin. Progress.

They arrived at her room, and Tate slid the card key into the slot. As the green lights flashed, a door opened on the hallway.

"You find your friend?" The woman from earlier stepped out of her room. "Whoa. Looks like she ordered a few bottles from room service after all."

"Yeah, thanks for your help." Tate hustled Blanca into the room and let the door slam behind them.

Blanca veered toward the sofa, but Tate held her upright. "Stay upright for a while and try to walk this off. Otherwise, you'll just fall asleep—and I need to know what happened."

She blinked several times and said, "Okay, okay."

The knots in Tate's gut loosened. He strode to the sliding glass door and dragged it open. The cool air that wafted into the room ruffled the drapes, and Tate walked Blanca to the fresh air. "Breathe deeply. You must've inhaled a ton of that chloroform to knock you out like that."

Blanca raised a hand to the back of her head and patted her hair. "Here. He hit me."

"I missed that." He positioned her next to the open door and placed her hand on the edge. He used his fingers to part her thick wavy hair and ran the tips along her scalp. He didn't feel any broken skin, but he did detect a small lump. "We need to get some ice on this."

She grabbed a handful of his hoodie. "Don't."

"I'm not leaving you. The door's locked and even if your attacker took your card key, the hotel attendant reprogrammed it and gave me another key. We're safe." He pulled her close and rubbed her back.

Blanca nestled closer to him, breathing deeply, her chest rising and falling against his, their hearts hammering out the same rhythm.

"I'm cold." She shifted out of his grasp, glancing down at her top, the water that had spilled down her front making the thin material cling to her breasts.

Tate shrugged out of his hoodie, warm from his body heat, and wrapped it around her. "How about some coffee? That might help."

"Yeah." She wriggled into the hoodie, slipping her arms in the sleeves and pulling it tight around her body. She licked her lips and then reached past him to chug some water from the bottle. "H-he attacked me in the ice-machine room."

Tate eased out a breath as he popped a pod into the coffee maker. "Can you start at the beginning?"

"I…" She scooped a hand through her hair and turned in a circle. Then she gasped and stumbled toward the coffee table.

Thinking she was going to collapse again, Tate jumped forward to grab her, but she spun around, her eyes wide, her arms flailing at her sides.

"The files. He stole the case files."

Chapter Eight

The sudden, swift movement made Blanca dizzy, and she placed a hand against Tate's broad chest to steady herself. She wouldn't mind sinking against that safe harbor again, but she had a big problem on her hands that cuddling with Tate wouldn't help.

"Whoa." He placed a hand on her hip. "Are you sure?"

Looking behind her, she stared at the empty spot on the floor next to the coffee table. "I left them right there. I never moved them. Oh God, he incapacitated me in the snack room, stole my room key and availed himself of those files."

"As long as you don't feel like you're going to pass out or go to sleep, have a seat. I'll get you some coffee and call the sheriff's department." He led her to the sofa as if she were a frail elderly person, and she sank down on the edge, not wanting to get engulfed by the soft cushions.

"Wait." She pushed the hair from her face and winced when her fingers met the sore spot on the back of her head. "You haven't called the police yet?

You found me passed out and didn't immediately call 911?"

"I…um." He kept his back to her as he poured some coffee. "You probably should drink this black."

He carried the mug of steaming liquid to her and placed it on the coffee table. Then he took his cell phone from his pocket and called the DFSD. After he explained the basics, he raised his eyebrows at her. "She seems fine, but maybe you can send an EMT to check her out."

Sipping the hot brew from the cup, she watched Tate over the rim.

He ended the call and said, "They're on the way. I'm hoping Richard downstairs has some footage of your attacker."

"So why is this your first call to the police?"

"You were out. I wasn't sure what happened."

She narrowed her eyes, which hurt the back of her eyeballs. "But even if it was an accident, you didn't think I might need assistance?"

"I'm sorry, Blanca. I just wanted to make sure it wasn't a case of…"

He spread his hands, and a light bulb went on in her foggy brain. "You thought I ODed or something?"

"Look, I just didn't know. I didn't want to embarrass you in case it was some kind of something gone wrong." His face reddened up to his naturally blond roots.

"Thanks, I guess. Not sure what kind of vibes I'm giving you if that's your first instinct."

"None. No. No vibes like that. I just wanted to protect you."

A little queasiness invaded her stomach, and it didn't have anything to do with the chloroform clapped over her nose and mouth. Had Tate heard something about her? Done a little digging?

"It's fine." She waved one hand in the air. "I'm pretty sure by the time you found me, the perpetrator was long gone. Why were you here again?"

"That can wait. Tell me from the beginning what happened."

"Got ready for bed." She plucked at the flannel material of her pajama bottoms. "Fancied a snack and made tracks for the vending machines on the fourth floor. Told you I had no self-control. Obviously, I didn't think I'd run into anything or I would've put more clothes on."

His gaze dipped to her chest, and she pulled his sweatshirt tighter.

"You didn't see or hear anyone?"

"Just a door behind me, but I didn't turn around." Her mouth dropped open. "Do you think it was someone staying on this floor?"

"I'm pretty sure that was your wine-swilling neighbor across the hall. She was putting her room-service tray outside. She's actually the one who told me you'd probably headed to the fourth-floor vending machines."

"Had I known this hotel had room service, that would've saved me a lot of trouble." She shot a look at the place where the boxes had been. "Got in the elevator, got to the fourth floor without seeing a soul and whipped out my card to get some cupcakes. While I was bending down to retrieve them, someone came at me. Thunked me on the head with something just enough to daze me and then went in for the kill with a chloroform-soaked cloth. He let me fall, and that's the last thing I remember before you poured water in my face."

"I didn't—I wasn't—that was for you to drink." He smacked a hand on the credenza and an inverted coffee cup rattled in its saucer. "He must've been watching you, waiting. If you hadn't come out of your room, maybe he would've broken in."

"Why take the boxes? How'd this person even know I had them?" She hunched her shoulders, Tate's sweatshirt not even offering enough warmth to ward off the chill snaking across her flesh.

"I told you, small town. That guy at the pizza place knew who you were." He snapped his fingers. "Who was that guy, anyway?"

"I have no clue. He didn't give me his card or anything. Ginger, though."

"What?" He jerked his head up.

"Redhead." She tapped her own dark locks. "He was kind of beefy, freckled, middle-aged and had red hair."

"Porter Monroe?" Tate dragged his knuckles across the sexy reddish-blond stubble on his chin.

"You know him?"

"I know Porter. There are a few redheads on

the island, but he works out with weights. Can't miss him."

"That could definitely be him." She slurped up more coffee. "Are you saying Porter Monroe followed me to the hotel, waited for you to leave and then looked for a way in?"

"I don't know if it was Porter, but that's exactly what someone did." Tate shoved his hands in his pockets. "I'm almost glad you did go out. What would he have done if he'd broken into your room and you caught him in the act?"

"I do sleep with my weapon under my pillow." She clapped a hand over her mouth. "Oh no. Is it still there? If someone stole my service weapon, I'm in deep trouble."

"Stay there. I'll check." A few seconds later he called from the other room. "Still here. He only wanted those boxes."

"But why?" Blanca clasped her hands between her knees.

"He doesn't want you reviewing the evidence. It could've been Jeremy's abductor." Tate massaged his neck.

"The Dead Falls Sheriff's Department is going to have the majority of those records online now, anyway." She leveled a gaze at him and gulped against her dry throat. "Aren't they?"

"Your guess is as good as mine. I'm not in law enforcement. I'm sure they're not going to tell me."

She groaned and touched her forehead to her knees. "This is gonna look so bad."

"It's not your fault, Blanca. You didn't leave your door unlocked with the files inside. You were assaulted."

A knock on the door made them both jump, and Tate made the first move to answer, and then opened it after verifying it was a deputy outside.

He swung open the door, and Blanca swallowed as two sheriff's deputies, Fletch and another guy, entered the room followed by two EMTs with a gurney.

"I don't need a ride to the emergency room. I'm fine."

Tate explained to them what happened as they swarmed her. "So check out the bump on her head and her vitals."

While the EMTs had her remove Tate's sweatshirt and recline on the sofa, Tate talked to the two deputies. The guy who wasn't Fletch pivoted and left the room.

Tate called to Blanca as the EMT wrapped the blood pressure cuff around her arm. "He's going to check the security footage."

"Take a deep breath, Blanca."

The silver cup on the stethoscope gave her a chill when he pressed it against her back, and she scooped in a large breath and released it on his command.

Fletch sauntered over. "Are you all right, Blanca? Did someone really steal Jeremy Ruesler's case files?"

"Unfortunately, yes." She made a grab for Tate's sweatshirt when the EMT stopped listening to her heart and lungs. How many times could she flash her breasts in one night?

"I'll have to report that to Sheriff Hopkins." Fletch rubbed his chin.

"I would expect you to, or I'll do it myself." She crossed her fingers. "Please, please, please tell me the department has the case files online. You didn't provide me with any physical evidence in those boxes, just paperwork and photos."

"We do—at least for current cases, and I seem to remember a lot of scanning going on a few years ago." Fletch scratched a point over his ear. "Why would someone want to steal that stuff?"

"Because someone doesn't want the FBI looking at the cold case." Tate touched the EMT's shoulder as he packed away his instruments. "Is she going to be okay?"

"She's fine. I'll leave some ibuprofen for the bump on her head, no broken skin. The chloroform is leaving her body." He turned to Blanca. "Keep drinking water. If you experience any other symptoms tonight, head to the ER."

"The only symptom I'm experiencing is embarrassment for losing those files."

The other deputy returned to the room. "Bad news."

"Don't tell me the hotel doesn't have security cameras. I've seen them." Tate folded his arms.

"Oh, they have them, but the floor cameras aren't working. Haven't worked for several months. The camera on the lobby doesn't show any activity, except you leaving around ten thirty and then coming back about forty-five minutes later."

"Side doors?"

"Don't work there, either, and the cameras on the parking lot picked up only a few guests. The clerk IDed them." The deputy shrugged.

Blanca snorted. "Are the cameras just for show, or what?"

"Don't know what to tell you, Agent Lopez. Security cameras didn't pick up your attacker. I also questioned a few people on this floor and the fourth, and nobody noticed anything unusual."

"Unbelievable. But he wouldn't have tried this stunt if he didn't think he could get away with it."

The deputies took a few more notes, and the EMT handed Blanca an ice pack before Tate shooed them all out of the room. Then he collapsed on the sofa beside her, rubbing his temple with two fingers. "How are you feeling?"

"Looks like you're the one who needs the ibuprofen." She jerked her thumb at her purse, undisturbed on the desk chair. "I have more in my bag if you want these."

"Has he been watching you? Us?"

Blanca curled one leg beneath her. "By *he*, do you mean Jeremy's kidnapper?"

"Who else? Who else would want those files?"

"A journalist, maybe? Perhaps someone's writing a big story, and they figured they could get all the details from the files for an exclusive."

"A journalist would hit you over the head and chloroform you to get a couple of boxes?"

She repositioned the ice pack on the back of her head. "They'd do it in DC."

He rolled his baby blues at her. "Do you need anything?"

Besides your strong arms around me again?

"Damn, I could use that cupcake." She snapped her fingers. "Or the pizza. I wouldn't object if you went out to your car and grabbed that pizza."

"I ate it."

She put her hands on her hips. "You took it home, ate it and then drove back here for some reason you haven't told me about yet."

"I never made it home. I stopped at the lookout for Dead Falls and ate it in the car, thought of something and then turned around to head back here." He rubbed her calf. "I'm glad I did."

Her eyelashes fluttered at the warm gush his touch sent coursing through her body. She could almost forgive him for eating all the pizza. "I'm glad, too. Thanks for helping me out and for having my back—just in case I was a secret chloroform-snorter on my off time."

A chuckle rumbled deep in his throat. "You have to admit, you know a lot more about me than I do about you."

"That's because you—" she leveled a finger at him "—are part of my case. I'm just the agent on the case. Big difference."

"Do you want that cupcake? It was still in the tray of the machine when I hauled you out of that room."

"That's all right. I don't want you to go out of your way when you leave."

"I'm not leaving."

"Excuse me?" A thrill ran through her body making her nipples tingle, and once again, she was grateful for his sweatshirt.

He patted the sofa. "I'm staying right here. What if you have some reaction tonight? What if the guy comes back after he decides the key to his identity is in those files after you've already gone through them?"

The thrill turned to a chill, and she hugged herself. "I seriously doubt that's going to happen, and you forgot I have a weapon. I actually know how to use it."

"I don't doubt it, but I'd feel better if you let me stay. I'll have another beer if you need to give me an excuse."

"Fine. I think there's an extra blanket in the closet, but after you bring me that cupcake you need to tell me why you came back here. What did you remember?"

He held up one finger. "Deal."

When Tate left the room, Blanca shrugged out of his hoodie and hung it on the back of a chair. Then she scurried into the bedroom and pulled a baggy Georgetown T-shirt over her skimpy camisole. Having him in the next room was going to be enough of a temptation. She didn't need to be parading around half-naked to add any more fuel to this fire kindling between them.

When he came back to the room, he tossed her the package of cupcakes, and she caught it with one hand, slightly squishing the contents. As she unwrapped the package, she said, "I hope these are worth it."

She bit into the chocolate and closed her eyes. "Totally worth it."

"More coffee?"

"No, thanks. I do eventually want to get to sleep tonight." She kicked her feet up on the coffee table. "Do you want the other one?"

"I don't know. You sacrificed a lot for that snack."

Using her toe, she scooted the plastic-wrapped cupcake to the edge of the table. "Go ahead. I sure as heck don't need it."

"You look great to me." He leaned over to snag the cupcake. "But if you're sure."

"Sit down and stop stalling." She licked a piece of chocolate frosting from her fingers. "Why'd you come back?"

He eased down to the edge of the table, his knees spread open, and bit into the cupcake. A dab of the cream in the center clung to his chin. "It's about Andrew Finnigan. The kid Porter mentioned to you in Luigi's. He disappeared in the mid-2000s, maybe 2010, about seven years after the incident with Jeremy."

"Disappeared, like never found again?" She tapped her chin, but Tate didn't take the hint.

"No, disappeared as in ran away and then was found dead on a ledge beneath the falls."

She put a hand to her throat. "How awful. How old was he?"

"About thirteen, I think. With some encouragement by the sheriff's department, the medical examiner ruled it an accident. Parents accepted it because it beat suicide."

"And? Why is it in question?"

"For me, it's mostly the condition of the body. He'd been out there for about a week, and there are plenty of wild animals on that ridge. It's unusual that none…fed on his body. Sorry."

"That is odd." She waved her hand at him. "You have a little bit of cream on your chin."

"Oh." He grabbed a napkin left over from the pizza and swiped it across his face. "And I know that info about Andrew isn't urgent, but I did try to call you, and you didn't answer. I thought that was strange, and then I got worried. I admit it."

"You don't have to apologize for being concerned about me." She popped the last bite of her cupcake into her mouth and dusted her fingers together. "Thanks again. I'm definitely going to look into the Andrew Finnigan case—if I'm still working Jeremy's cold one."

"Don't see how your bosses can blame you. You left the boxes in a locked hotel room."

"Let's just say I don't have the best track record with the agents in charge." She stood up, brushing crumbs from her pajama bottoms. "I'll find you that blanket. I'm afraid I don't have a toothbrush for you, though."

"That's okay. I'll use my finger and swish some water around in my mouth."

"That'll work." She pushed up from the sofa and slid open the mirrored closet door.

"I'll get that." Tate had come up behind her and reached up to get the blanket folded on the top shelf.

She stepped back from the warm invitation of his body. "I'll brush my teeth and leave my toothpaste on the sink for you."

"Thanks." He hugged the blanket to his chest and pivoted toward the sitting room.

Blanca dipped into the bathroom, brushed her teeth and splashed some water on her face. She could probably do with another shower after napping on the floor next to the ice machine, but the night's events had hit her like a sledgehammer and her head ached. She capped the toothpaste and left it on the counter, and then slid into the bedroom without looking at Tate.

She snapped the door behind her, dragged the T-shirt over her head and crawled into bed, feeling for the gun beneath her pillow. Too bad she hadn't taken it with her to the snack machine.

She snuggled under the covers as she heard the water running in the bathroom. What had been the real reason for Tate returning to the hotel? Had he really been worried about her?

A smile curled her lips, and she closed her eyes. It had been a long time since someone had been worried about her safety, and it felt good. Too good.

Chapter Nine

What felt like several seconds later, Blanca rolled to her side to the sound of more water in the bathroom. Was Tate in the shower now?

She rubbed her eyes and squinted at the green numbers floating beside the bed. She knew it couldn't be seven thirty at night, so it must be morning.

She didn't want Tate to catch her sleeping in, so she scooted from the bed. She yanked her phone off the charger and dropped the T-shirt over her head as she padded to the bedroom door. She peeked into the sitting room and blinked at the light pouring in from the window, laying stripes on the sofa and the blanket folded neatly on one cushion.

She crossed the room to the credenza and slid in a pod for some coffee. She rinsed out her cup from last night in case Tate wanted a cup. As the coffee dripped into the cup, Blanca took a deep breath and checked her messages.

Nothing from her boss, Crandall. Either Sheriff Hopkins hadn't heard about the missing files yet, or he hadn't had time to call Crandall. Maybe Hopkins hadn't heard about them himself. It would probably be best if she told the sheriff first. She should've mentioned that to the deputies last night.

"Anything new?"

She jumped at the sound of Tate's voice behind her and spun around, clutching the phone in her hand. She almost dropped it when she got an eyeful of Tate sluicing wet hair back from his face, a towel hanging dangerously low on his hips.

She took a shallow breath and squeaked, "You seem to be missing some clothes."

"Sorry. I left them out here. Didn't think you'd be up this early. I probably woke you up, huh?" He whipped the towel off his body and bunched it in one hand as he sauntered past her, smelling like a juicy piece of citrus fruit.

Her heart skipped a few beats and then returned to its normal pace when she saw the boxers beneath the towel—but just barely. She somehow kept her tongue from hanging out of her mouth as he shook out his jeans, his back to her, and flashed those shifting plates of muscle. He pulled on his pants and tugged his shirt over his head before turning around, but not before she caught sight of his six-pack as it dipped into his jeans.

She nodded toward the credenza. "Coffee? I made a cup for myself, using the mug from last night, but there's another, clean one."

"Sure, I'll take a cup. How are you feeling?"

"I feel fine. No lingering effects from either the chloroform or the bump on the head." She dumped some creamer and sweetener into her cup and swirled the liquid with a stir stick.

"Any idea what he used to hit you?"

"None. It was hard and solid, and he needed only one blow to take me down so he could finish the job with the chloroform."

He chewed his lip. "Definitely a man, though."

"Definitely." She shoved another pod into the coffee maker and put the remaining cup beneath the dispenser. "Could be a relative."

"A relative of the kidnapper?"

"Jeremy was taken almost twenty years ago. How old would his abductor have to be today?" She sipped the coffee, inhaling the scent, and cupping it on her tongue before swallowing.

"Are you kidding?" Tate spread his hands. "He could've been twenty then, forty now, like Porter. Thirty then, fifty now, and everything in between. You think he's too old to get up to his old tricks? Does someone like that ever stop? Maybe he moved away and came back."

"I don't know, Tate. How could he be hiding in plain sight?"

"You went through the FBI academy. You know better than most. If they looked like monsters and stood out to the rest of us, they wouldn't be able to act on their evil."

"I know." She let the last few drips of coffee land in the mug and asked, "Cream or sugar?"

"Black is fine. I'll gulp some down, and then I have to get going. We have some training today."

He took the cup from her, his fingers brushing hers. "What are your plans for the day?"

"I have a feeling I'll be spending most of the day at the sheriff's station—explaining to Hopkins what happened to his files and hopefully going through the online version. I also plan to do a little research on Andrew Finnigan's case. His parents still here?"

"Long gone." He slurped some coffee and set the cup down. He dropped onto the sofa and pulled on his socks and boots. "I'll check in on you at the end of the day to see how you're feeling. Anything seems off, head to the hospital."

"I will." As he got up and took another sip of coffee, she handed his sweatshirt to him. "Thanks again for everything last night—the beer and pizza, too, although that seems ages ago now."

"Yeah, it does." He held the sweatshirt to his face for a second before shaking his head and slipping into it. He paused at the open door. "Take it easy today."

"Will do." Blanca closed the door behind him with a sigh. Why did the grown-up Tate Mitchell have to be so hot?

She showered and put on one of her pantsuits. She needed all the professionalism she could muster today.

Tooling into the station, she hoped that she could reach Sheriff Hopkins before the bad news did. She nodded to a few of the deputies she saw at the search for Noah the other night and pointed down the hallway toward Hopkins's office. "Is he in?"

With permission from the deputy at the front desk,

Blanca squared her shoulders and strode toward the sheriff's office. She rapped on the open door. "Sheriff Hopkins?"

"Come in, come in. I was expecting you, Agent Lopez."

Her stomach sank to her toes. "Oh? You heard about the…incident last night at my hotel?"

"I did." He waved her into his office. "Are you okay?"

"I'm fine. I'm sorry about those files, though. Totally unacceptable." She cleared her throat through his silence. "I'm hoping you have most of those online, so I can continue my research."

He steepled his fingers and peered at her over the tips. "We have most of the witness statements online. I'm not sure about the photos, though. We'll give you access to the database, so you can look."

She eked out a small breath, trying not to collapse with relief. "Good to hear that. What's not good is that I think Jeremy's kidnapper or a family member may have stolen the evidence. Who else would go through that much trouble to get the files?"

"I wouldn't jump to conclusions, Agent Lopez. It could've been anyone, really." He flicked his fingers. "Bloggers, you know, those podcast people. Some true-crime nut. Teenage troublemakers. Maybe even Ruesler family members hoping to get some inside info they think we left out."

She widened her eyes. "You think Birdie Ruesler attacked me to look at evidence regarding her son's disappearance?"

"Birdie's not Jeremy's only living relative. He has a sister. His dad isn't on the island, but he's in the vicinity."

"Maybe." She didn't want to argue with Hopkins before asking a favor. "In addition to looking at the Ruesler case online, I'd like to have a look at the files for the Andrew Finnigan case, accidental death at the falls, around 2010, I believe."

"Finnigan?" He scratched his chin. "I remember that case—runaway. May have been a suicide, but the medical examiner ruled it accidental. Why do you think that's connected to the Ruesler case?"

"Some irregularities with the body." She clasped her hands in her lap. "Is it okay?"

"Sure, sure. I'm going to send you to Deputy Amanda Robard. She's our current computer whiz, and she's two doors down." He dropped his gaze to the Danish on his desktop. "Anything else?"

Did the guy actually do anything in this office other than eat?

"That's all. Just wanted to apologize for losing the files." She stood up, hitching her purse over her shoulder. "I'll take care of notifying my supervisor, Agent Crandall."

"Sure, sure. Not your fault, Agent Lopez. I'm sorry you were attacked in our little town." He scooped up his Danish with one hand, pausing it halfway to his open mouth. "I understand you were with Tate Mitchell at the time."

She stopped at the door, pinning her purse against her side. "Not exactly. I questioned him in my hotel room about the night Jeremy disappeared. He left, forgot something and returned to find me conked out next to the ice machine."

He mumbled around chews. "Did he tell you anything?"

"No." She made a quick pivot out of his office. The FBI kept things from the local law all the time. Why should she be the exception?

She stopped two offices down from Hopkins's and barged in on a female deputy, her dark hair pulled into a tight bun to complement her crisp uniform.

"Deputy Robard? I'm FBI Special Agent Blanca Lopez. We met the other night during the search for Noah."

Robard looked up and squinted. "Oh yeah. FBI. You can call me Amanda."

"And you can call me Blanca." She jerked her thumb toward Hopkins's office. "The Sheriff told me you could get me into the database. There are a couple of cases I want to research."

"I heard about what happened last night." Amanda tapped her head. "You okay?"

Blanca slumped against the wall. "Who didn't hear about the incident last night?"

"Small town. Local kid working the front desk." Amanda shrugged. "Stuff gets around."

"Except who kidnapped Jeremy Ruesler and snatched Noah Fielding—*that* stuff doesn't get around."

"I know, right?" Amanda kicked a chair on wheels out toward her. "Have a seat, and I'll get you a login. You can work in here. I just finished."

Blanca wheeled the chair next to Amanda, who took her through the log-in process to the database and showed her how to do a search.

When she finished, Amanda grabbed her coffee cup and pushed back from the desk. "You were with Tate last night?"

Uh-oh. Was she stepping on an ex's toes? Or a wannabe love interest?

"Just professional. I had a lot of questions for him regarding the Ruesler case."

Amanda laughed. "I don't care if you wanna jump his bones. I'm not into dudes. Just know that Tate's wound pretty tightly, despite his easy-breezy demeanor and success with the girlies. Don't know how much you can get out of him. He doesn't wanna remember that night, even though he pretends he does."

"Thanks for the tip." Blanca willed the hot blush rushing up her throat to back down. Was her attraction to Tate that obvious?

As she left the office, Amanda said, "Just make sure you log-out when you're done and close the door behind you. It locks automatically."

"Thanks."

As soon as Blanca heard Amanda's footsteps retreat down the hall, she jumped up and closed the door. She'd prefer privacy. Seemed like you couldn't keep anything a secret in this town.

She accessed the Ruesler file first, just to make sure she could. She released a breath, as she discovered most of the paperwork that had been stolen last night had already been entered online; even the photos had been scanned. Her attacker's actions hadn't accomplished what he'd wanted—whatever that was.

She perused the file for over an hour, taking notes, before doing a search for the Finnigan case.

That case had been more recent, and it too was all online. She clicked through the notes and even did a search for various forms of the word *whistle*, but nothing popped up.

She pressed her fingers to her lips as she brought up the pictures of Andrew's dead body. She hoped his parents hadn't seen these, but Tate had been right. The boy's body looked fairly pristine for being out in the wild for almost a week.

She'd seen bodies that had been in the elements for more than a day or two, and they usually displayed evidence of animal activity. No wildlife had bothered to investigate Andrew's body near a forest with actual wild animals?

What did that mean, exactly? Maybe he'd been hiding in those caves behind the falls before deciding to kill himself or before slipping from the outcropping. Just because law enforcement couldn't find Andrew, it didn't mean he wasn't alive out there while they were looking for him. Surely, it didn't mean he'd been killed elsewhere and thrown from the falls. Would it even be possible for someone to get a dead body up there? The ME had indicated that Andrew had been dead for several days. Could he have been mistaken, given the temperature?

She brought up the clearest photo of the boy's entire body and zoomed in on different parts. She enlarged his hands and leaned forward, spotting an injury on his wrist.

Her heart skipped a beat when she zoomed in on his other wrist. The same mark appeared in the same place as the other one. She snagged a still of both wrists and transferred the photo to another app where she could focus and clarify the image.

When she finished her manipulations of the photo, she sat back in her chair and sucked in her bottom lip. The marks on Andrew's wrists were from restraints.

Someone had been holding Andrew somewhere before killing him. This was no accidental death.

Chapter Ten

Tate cranked on the warm water and stood under the spray as the soot and dirt from his body ran down the drain. Training had felt extra hard today, or maybe it was the pizza and beer from last night—or his restless sleep.

The narrow sofa in Blanca's hotel room hadn't helped, but it was Blanca's presence in the next room that had made sleep so elusive. Any other time, any other situation, any other woman and he'd have been making moves to get into her bed.

She'd been injured, woozy. No way he would've taken advantage of that with any woman, but especially not Blanca. Something about their interactions seemed…different. Every encounter with her made him feel as if he were standing on the edge of some precipice. If he made one wrong move, he could fall and be banished from her presence forever.

Aaron jabbed at the plastic shower curtain and shouted, "Dude, could you save some water for the rest of us. What are you doing in there?"

"You should know, Huang. Why are you spying

on me?" Tate turned off the water and grabbed his towel hanging over the curtain rod.

He dried off quickly, wrapped the towel around his waist and stepped into the locker room. The agency didn't have enough showers for all the crew members, although some elected to drive home in their filthy uniforms after training to shower in the privacy of their own homes. The married people tended to do that more than the singles, as they had spouses and kids waiting for them.

Tate had never been interested in that life, and the thought of having kids terrified him. He'd never forget what losing Jeremy had done to the Rueslers. Birdie had been the best mom on the island among his friends' mothers. Baked the best cookies. Told the funniest jokes. Knew all the cool music. The woman he'd seen yesterday was a shell of the one he'd known as a child.

He shoved his dirty uniform in a bag and finished dressing. When he checked his phone on the way out, the message notification from Blanca put a spring in his step. He threw his bag in the back seat of his Jeep and tapped on her message.

She'd found something and wanted him to call her. He blew out a breath. At least she hadn't been re-called from the case for the missing files. He started the engine but stayed in Park, buzzing down a window.

He placed the call, and she answered almost immediately. He said, "Got your text. What's up?"

"First of all, Hopkins didn't seem too upset that

the files were stolen, and most of the paperwork and photos are online. So I lucked out there. Secondly, I got into Andrew Finnigan's case, and I saw something on his photos."

"What did you see?" He took a gulp of water from the bottle in his cup holder.

"Marks on his wrist. Tate, it looks as if Andrew had been restrained. I checked the autopsy report, and the medical examiner made a note of abrasions on the wrists but didn't make any connection to the boy being manacled."

Tate pushed up the sleeve of his jacket on his left arm and stared at his own wrist. The marks on his wrists had lasted for days where Jeremy's abductor had tied him up. His body had been lashed to the trunk of a tree, but his hands and feet had been bound, as well.

"Tate? Don't you think that's important?"

"I do, yeah. It's strange they didn't make a bigger deal out of it, but I know they were quick to settle on accidental." He rubbed his wrist.

"Settle on accidental to avoid a determination of suicide, but why rush to accidental if it was homicide?"

"I don't know, Blanca. You can question Hopkins, but he'd just started around that time. Maddox was the sheriff then, and he's dead."

"How about the medical examiner?" He heard some papers rustle over the line. "Dr. Scott Summers?"

"Summers? Yeah, I think he still lives on the island, but he's retired."

"One Minute" Survey

You get up to **FOUR** books <u>and</u> a Mystery Gift...

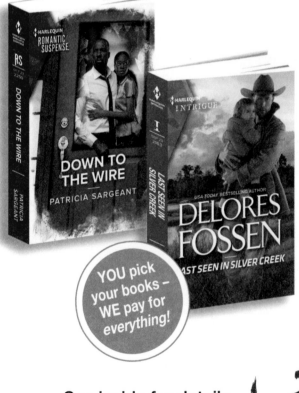

Dear Reader,

Your opinions are important to us. So if you'll participate in our fast and free "One Minute" Survey, YOU can pick up to four wonderful books that WE pay for when you try the Harlequin Reader Service!

As a leading publisher of women's fiction, we'd love to hear from you. That's why we promise to reward you for completing our survey.

IMPORTANT: Please complete the survey and return it. We'll send your Free Books and a Free Mystery Gift right away. And we pay for shipping and handling too! *We pay for EVERYTHING!*

Try **Harlequin® Romantic Suspense** and get 2 books featuring heart-racing page-turners with unexpected plot twists and irresistible chemistry that will keep you guessing to the very end.

Try **Harlequin Intrigue® Larger-Print** and get 2 books featuring action-packed stories that will keep you on the edge of your seat. Solve the crime and deliver justice at all costs.

Or TRY BOTH!

Thank you again for participating in our "One Minute" Survey. It really takes just a minute (or less) to complete the survey… and your free books and gift will be well worth it!

If you continue with your subscription, you can look forward to curated monthly shipments of brand-new books from your selected series, always at a discount off the cover price! Plus you can cancel any time. So don't miss out, return your One Minute Survey today to get your Free books.

Pam Powers

"One Minute" Survey

GET YOUR FREE BOOKS AND A FREE GIFT!
✓ Complete this Survey ✓ Return this survey

1 Do you try to find time to read every day?
☐ YES ☐ NO

2 Do you prefer stories with suspensful storylines?
☐ YES ☐ NO

3 Do you enjoy having books delivered to your home?
☐ YES ☐ NO

4 Do you share your favorite books with friends?
☐ YES ☐ NO

YES! I have completed the above "One Minute" Survey. Please send me my Free Books and a Free Mystery Gift (worth over $20 retail). I understand that I am under no obligation to buy anything, as explained on the back of this card.

☐ **Harlequin®
Romantic
Suspense**
240/340 CTI G2AD

☐ **Harlequin
Intrigue®
Larger-Print**
199/399 CTI G2AD

☐ **BOTH**
240/340 & 199/399
CTI G2AE

FIRST NAME

LAST NAME

ADDRESS

APT.#

CITY

STATE/PROV.

ZIP/POSTAL CODE

EMAIL ☐ Please check this box if you would like to receive newsletters and promotional emails from Harlequin Enterprises ULC and its affiliates. You can unsubscribe anytime.

HI/HRS-1123-OM

"Wait. I know that name." Blanca clicked her tongue. "He was at the search for Noah. He was in our group, so he's still active, at least. The fact that he's retired doesn't matter. I have his autopsy report. I can show it to him and see if he remembers anything about the case. I don't see on the report that he ever provided an explanation for the marks on Andrew's wrists, but maybe he remembers the reason for that."

Tate massaged his temple with his knuckle. "So what does this mean to you? Do you think Jeremy was held before he was…murdered? I don't believe there was anything near the bones to indicate that, but I'm no forensic scientist."

"I suppose we'll find out. We haven't even gotten the DNA results back. But what this might mean?" She paused and took a sip of something. "Maybe Noah Fielding isn't dead, yet. Maybe he's being held somewhere, like Andrew was. He might still have a chance."

"Like Andrew *maybe* was. You don't know that."

"You're right, but that's what I'm here for."

"You're still here. How'd your boss back in DC react to the missing files?"

She cleared her throat. "I haven't heard from him, yet."

"Shouldn't you tell him yourself?"

"Yeah, yeah. I will. I just wanted to make sure Dead Falls had the files online. That way, I can give Crandall a good news-bad news situation." She giggled, and Tate could tell she was nervous about talking to her boss.

She'd made a couple of references about being in the doghouse with upper command but hadn't gone into any detail about it. He could imagine her going rogue now and then, but she seemed dedicated to the job…and good at it.

"No ill effects from last night?"

"No. I feel great today."

Obviously, she hadn't tossed and turned like he had. "Free for dinner? To, uh, discuss the cases."

"Sure. Takeout at my hotel again?"

"We do actually have restaurants in Dead Falls, you know."

"I know that, but maybe it's best if we're not seen out together. I don't know."

Tate furrowed his brow. "All right, but how about my place instead of your hotel? If anyone's creeping around the cabin, I'll know about it."

"Didn't you have training today? You shouldn't have to go home and cook."

He snorted. "What gave you the impression I cooked? The most I can handle is barbecue, but Astrid left some food in the freezer. I think she has some lasagna in there. I can make a salad."

"Perfect. I'll bring the red wine and dessert."

And just like that, he had something and someone to go home to like some of the other guys.

He ended the call, and his lead foot got him home in record time. He'd already showered, so he dumped his uniform, along with some other clothes, in the washing machine and ran a critical eye over his space. Some areas were neater without his nephew around, but some decidedly needed work before Blanca got here.

By the time he heard her car in his driveway, he'd put the breakfast dishes in the dishwasher, wiped the crumbs from the counter, swept the kitchen floor and put the lasagna in the oven.

He opened the door with a flourish, and Blanca greeted him with two plastic bags swinging in her hands. "I hope you like cabernet sauvignon and ice cream."

"Together?" He took the bags from her hands and winked.

Wedging her hands on her curvy hips, she tilted her head at him.

"What?" He raised his eyebrows.

"Nothing." She sniffed the air. "Garlic two nights in a row. Nobody is going to want to get too close to me."

"I, um…" The words died on his lips, and he pivoted toward the kitchen, bringing the bags with him. She hadn't seemed to appreciate the wink, so he should probably cool the flirty act. "You'll like Astrid's lasagna. She's a good cook."

Blanca followed him into the kitchen and ran her hand along the quartz counter. "Anyone could be a good cook in this kitchen."

He glanced over his shoulder at her as he uncorked the wine to let it breathe. "Do you cook much?"

"I have my phases, especially when I'm trying

to eat healthy. Then a big case comes up, and I'm grabbing fast food." She shrugged. "You said you had stuff for a salad. I *can* do that."

"Sure." He pointed to the fridge. "You can grab some veggies from the crisper. Olly doesn't like cooked vegetables, so Astrid makes him eat raw ones. A lot of those are still good."

"Has your sister always lived here with you?" She bent forward to open the crisper drawer, and he shifted his gaze away from her luscious derriere before she caught him.

"No, just since the divorce. Her ex is a jerk with violent tendencies, so she took refuge here."

"Lot of those running around." Blanca dumped several plastic bags on the countertop and slid a knife from the block. She held it up to the light and ran a finger along the blade, which glinted.

Tate held up his hands. "I swear, that's not me—at least not the violent part."

The side of her mouth lifted. "At least you're honest—with others."

He almost dropped the wineglass he'd just slid from the shelf. "What is that supposed to mean?"

"I talked to your friend Amanda today."

"Oh, Amanda. She's in the wrong line of work. She should be a therapist, and then she could actually charge for all that advice she's always handing out."

Blanca started chopping the vegetables with quick, precise strokes. "You know her theory about you?"

"I do, but she's wrong. I already helped you with

the case, right? I remembered the whistling, and I told you about Andrew." He poured the ruby-red liquid into the first glass where it shimmered.

"That's true." She held up the knife, a piece of carrot stuck to the side of the blade. "But Porter Monroe's the one who told me about Andrew Finnigan."

"Yeah." He poured another glass of wine and ran his finger along the neck of the bottle to catch a drop. He sucked it off.

She stopped dicing. "Yeah, what?"

"I mean, why did he approach you? Especially about the cold case. I could see if he had something pertinent to add to the search for Noah Fielding."

"Not sure. What are you thinking?" She used the knife to slide the veggies into the two bowls of lettuce.

"Just seems odd. Law enforcement looked into Porter when Jeremy went missing." Tate rubbed his chin. That's another thing that had come back to him out of the blue, and he couldn't remember seeing that in the files last night.

"Really?" The knife and cutting board clattered in the sink where Blanca dropped them. "Why? He hardly looks old enough."

"He was about twenty at the time. Very big youth volunteer."

Blanca narrowed her eyes. "He was? Like scouts and stuff like that?"

"Uh-huh. He knew us boys. He knew a lot of boys, still does."

"Is he married with kids of his own now?"

"He's married with one daughter, but he wasn't at the time. He played football in high school and started helping the coaches out. It began with that." The timer for the oven beeped, and he grabbed an oven mitt. "I don't know. Just forget it."

"Why would I forget that?"

He opened the oven door and a blast of heat hit his face. "I don't like the idea of accusing someone with no proof. A good friend of mine served time for a crime he didn't commit, just because of appearances."

"That's terrible, but sometimes where there's smoke, there's fire." She set the bowls on the kitchen table where he'd put out a couple of place mats and silverware. "I can take a look at him, and he won't even know it."

"Be subtle." As he placed the pan on top of the stove and cut into the layers of meat, cheese and pasta, he felt eyes boring into his back. Without even turning around, he asked, "What?"

"I didn't see anything about Porter Monroe in the files—not last night, not today when I went through them more thoroughly."

He turned toward her, the two plates loaded with food in his hands. "I didn't, either."

"You remembered, didn't you? All this poking around is jostling those memories in your brain."

"Probably." He brushed past her on his way to the table. "But like I told you before, I know I didn't see Jeremy's abductor. If I had and could ID him, he would never have left me alive. There was no way at the time when he captured me and tied me up that he would've known I'd suffer from memory loss. He knew then I wouldn't be able to pick him out."

"He must've been wearing a mask. It was winter, chilly outside. He wouldn't have looked odd to anyone for wearing a balaclava or beanie and scarf in that weather, right?" She pulled out a chair and sat at the table, pinching the stem of her wineglass between her fingers.

He clinked his glass with hers. "Or I didn't get a look at him at all. He could've knocked me out from a distance or snuck up behind me. I was unconscious when he dragged me to the tree and tied me to it. He then slipped away."

"Where was Jeremy all this time when he was dealing with you?"

"Incapacitated, maybe...dead." Tate pinched the bridge of his nose and then took a long draw from his glass. The wine's warm trickle down his throat didn't do anything for his sudden headache, but he felt the ease in his muscles.

"I don't think he killed Jeremy there, Tate. There was no murder scene, no body. And if he was going to kill Jeremy, he would've killed you, too." She swirled her wine in the glass. "No, he took him. Just like he took Andrew Finnigan and now Noah Fielding."

"You're making some leaps here." He cut into his lasagna, the cheese that oozed from the side making his stomach feel queasy. Or was it the thought that someone had imprisoned these boys before killing them that had turned his stomach? "Why didn't the sheriff's department investigate the marks on Andrew's wrists?"

"I have no clue, but you can bet I'm going to track down Dr. Scott Summers, the medical examiner, to find out." She chewed and patted her lips with a napkin. "This lasagna is so good. Give my compliments to Astrid."

"I will." He ran the tines of his fork through the tomato sauce on his plate. "Is this cold case a plum job for you or busywork to get you out of the way?"

She stopped midchew and clenched her fork as if ready to kill her dinner. "You get right to the point, huh?"

"It just feels as if there's an imbalance here—you know so much about me, and I know nothing about you."

"There's supposed to be an imbalance, Tate. I'm the investigator, and you're the witness." She dropped her fork and grabbed her wineglass, draining it.

Pointing his fork at the glass, he asked, "Do you want another?"

"Our positions are reversed tonight." She pinged her empty glass with her fingernail. "I'd love another glass, but I have to drive back to my hotel on dark, unfamiliar roads. The last thing I need here on Dead Falls is a DUI."

"Same solution as last night. You can stay the night here—in the guest room if you choose to... indulge."

Blanca's eyes burned with a dark intensity that made him feel drunker than if he'd downed the rest of the bottle himself. Was he really suggesting that she spend the night? He needed to be careful here. If he got involved with Blanca, he didn't think he'd be able to extricate himself as easily as he'd done from other relationships.

She lodged the tip of her tongue in the corner of her mouth, and Tate's heart pounded with expectation and excitement.

When her cell phone rang, he blinked. He almost told her to forget it, but she glanced at the display and held up her finger.

"It's my contact at the FBI lab." She wiped her hands and tapped the phone once to answer and then again, as she showed him she was putting the caller on Speaker.

"Hi, Gwen. Do you have the results on the bones?"

"I do, Blanca."

Tate tensed his muscles, his mouth suddenly dry.

"I'm afraid it's not good news…or maybe it is." Gwen coughed. "The bones we found are not a match for Jeremy Ruesler."

The roaring in Tate's ears subsided, and he gripped the edge of the table.

Blanca widened her eyes at him. "I can't believe it. Birdie Ruesler's DNA isn't a match for the bones?"

"Nope, but there's more."

Tate shifted his aching jaw from side to side.

"The bones do belong to a young male—not a child but not an adult."

"Older than Jeremy?" Blanca put her wineglass to her lips, obviously forgetting she'd finished it.

"A little older. This boy was about fifteen years old and, based on certain characteristics of the skull, Native American. Further, we can date the bones from about 2012 to 2018."

Blanca blew out a breath. "Okay, thanks, Gwen. You'll send me the full report?"

Tate had stopped listening to Blanca's conversation, as the roaring had returned to his ears.

Blanca ended the call and cocked her head. "Are you okay?"

Tate muttered through dry lips, "It's Gabe White-cotton."

Chapter Eleven

Blanca's disappointment surged into confusion and renewed excitement as her heart pounded so hard it made the buttons on her sweater quiver. "Who is Gabe Whitecotton? I haven't heard that name before."

Tate tossed off the rest of his wine and jumped from his chair to take a turn around the kitchen, clasping the back of his neck in a gesture becoming familiar to her. "That's because he was listed as a runaway. He's from the Samish nation. Lived on the reservation across the river."

Folding her arms, she dug her fingernails into her biceps. "Why were the authorities so sure he was a runaway? Because of the age?"

"It had nothing to do with his age, Blanca. He disappeared when he was thirteen around 2017."

"But Gwen just told me the bones belong to a fifteen-year-old." She stopped and placed her hands over her mouth.

"Exactly." Tate punched a fist into his palm. "Where was he for those two years?"

"Maybe—" she planted her hands on either side

of her plate, fingers spread "—Gwen's estimate is off. Maybe the bones are from a twelve-year-old."

"She sounded confident to me. I'm pretty sure there are measurements and other tests they perform to pinpoint the age." He grabbed the wine bottle by the neck. "Why are you trying to talk yourself out of your own theory? This would match with the marks on Andrew's wrists. It would explain why Jeremy's body has never been found—to this day."

With an unsteady hand, she held out her glass for a pour. "Jeremy in 2003, Andrew in 2010, Gabe you think in 2017, and now Noah. Are there more? Does every missing boy from the Discovery Bay islands in the past twenty, thirty years have to be reinvestigated?"

Tate shook his head as he added a steady stream of red liquid to her glass. So much for staying sober.

"Why were the authorities so quick to call Gabe a runaway?"

Rubbing his eyes, Tate slumped back in his chair. "He'd done it before. I had just finished my training around that time and had moved back to the island, so I remember the case."

She studied his face, his jaw a straight, hard line despite his relaxed position in the chair. She'd bet that he remembered that case…and every other case of boys gone missing. He'd pulled Gabe's name and date missing right out of his brain as soon as Gwen had provided the details.

"Gabe had a troubled home life, had skipped out a few times…and he lived on the reservation." Tate rolled his shoulders. "Hate to say it, but Sheriff Maddox was more likely to gloss over a case when it involved the Samish."

"Sounds to me like he glossed over a lot of cases."

Tate hung his head and covered his face with his hands. "I was dreading the news but needed the closure. I can't imagine how Birdie's going to feel when she finds out the bones don't match Jeremy's."

"I'll tell her myself. No point in putting yourself through that again." Blanca pushed back from her chair and crossed to Tate's side of the table. She squeezed his shoulder. "I'm sorry. I really thought you had found Jeremy."

He glanced up, dropping his hands to his lap. "What now? Are you going to be pulled from the case? The FBI sent you out here to investigate the cold case of Jeremy Ruesler's disappearance and the discovery of his bones. Those aren't Jeremy's bones. Now what?"

"I'll present the rest of this information to my boss. It really looks like we have a serial killer here. And there's Noah Fielding." She took a gulp of wine. She couldn't leave now, even if she wanted to—and she really didn't want to.

Tate scratched his chin. "Whatever we *believe*, there's no clear evidence that any of these boys are linked. Noah could've gotten lost on a walk. That blood on his hat could've been from anything."

"I think once I tell my boss about all the cases, he'll see it my way."

"It's important to you, isn't it?" Tate crossed his

arms and tipped back in his chair. "Why does this case mean so much to you?"

Besides giving her more time to explore all the sides of Tate Mitchell? She cleared her throat and took another swig of wine. "I need a win here. I have to prove myself to the agency, to my boss."

"I figured that, Blanca, but why? Did you accidentally shoot someone? Seriously get on the wrong side of someone important?"

"Worse. I slept with someone." She downed the rest of her wine and grabbed the bottle. Might as well go all in.

Tate's head jerked up, and a slow smile spread across his face. "If that were all, a lot of us would be in a lot of trouble."

Her lips twitched. "It wasn't some random person. He was my mentor at the agency, Manny Rodriguez."

"Ah, so he sexually harassed you in the workplace, and *you're* the one in trouble." He clicked his tongue. "Sounds about right."

"Ugh." She ran her fingers through her hair. "It's more complicated than that. He was married and didn't tell me. He also tried to control my career. Everyone knew I was Manny's protégée. When he found out we were about to be discovered, he went to the brass first and confessed, but he put his own twist on it. He said I offered him sex in exchange for promoting my career, even though I knew he was married."

"Jerk." He clasped his hands together. "End of the

day, he was having an extramarital relationship with someone he was supervising."

"Yeah, well, he got reprimanded, but my reputation took the hit. In some circles, the situation only served to embellish his." She sighed, propped her elbow on the table and sunk her chin into her hand. "I blame myself. He had me starry-eyed, and I did have definite perks being in his orbit. But that's *not* why I slept with him."

"Why did you? Because he was such a great guy?" Tate snorted, but she could tell he'd aimed his derision at Manny, not her.

"It's hard to explain. Manny was—*is* a superstar in the agency. When he took an interest in me— purely professional at first—I was flattered. I don't know how I fell into his trap. He's a smooth talker."

"I know the type." He wiggled his eyebrows at her. "You don't have to explain. My sister fell for the same kind of guy, and that ended badly."

"Anyway—" she ran a finger along the rim of her glass "—me out here is kind of my exile and my redemptive moment at the same time. I have to prove that my meteoric rise in the agency was not the result of Manny's favoritism."

"And you do that by solving Jeremy's case."

"All of them, Tate. I'm going to solve every damned one of them. Someone is taking boys here on Dead Falls, and I'm going to catch him."

"You're not going to do it tonight. You're not even getting back on the road tonight." He pinged the almost empty bottle of wine with his fingernail. "You've almost polished off that whole bottle yourself."

She sucked in her bottom lip, which had all the fruity hints of the wine. After what she'd just told him, would he think she'd done this on purpose? "I—I can leave my car here and call for a cab."

"Out here? You'd be lucky to find one in the radius in the next hour." He pointed to the ceiling. "You've already been in the spare room. It's all set up."

She stretched her arms over her head. Could she manage to spend the night in the room next to this man again without making a move? Maybe if she stuck to business.

She cleared her throat. "Is there any way we can prove those bones belong to Gabe? Does he still have family here?"

"His parents are gone, but he still has relatives living. You shouldn't have any problem getting DNA samples from them." He rose from the table and picked up their plates. "I can go with you, and nobody is going to run me off their property this time."

"Mrs. Ruesler doesn't really blame you. You were a child then. There's nothing you could've done."

"I know that, but I always did wonder, and she probably does too, why the guy grabbed Jeremy and not me."

"Like we said before—convenience. He probably spotted Jeremy first. He didn't want both of you, so he left you there unable to identify him." She scooped up the salad bowls and followed him to the sink. "Let me rinse the dishes and put them in the dishwasher. You can take care of the rest."

While she scraped the remains of their meal down the garbage disposal and loaded the dishwasher, Tate wrapped up the rest of the lasagna and put it in the fridge.

He bumped her hip as he put the pan under the water and added some soap. "I do actually have an extra toothbrush you can use, courtesy of my dentist."

"I'm set. Don't worry about me. I'll crash in the spare room. With all that food and adrenaline, though, I barely feel buzzed."

"Don't even think about driving back to your hotel."

"Oh, don't worry."

"When are you going to give Mrs. Ruesler the news?" Tate finished wiping the lasagna pan and flicked the dish towel over his shoulder.

"Tomorrow, first thing, before she hears from another source." She held up her hand to tick off her fingers. "Then I'm going to contact Dr. Summers and head to the Samish reservation to track down Gabe Whitecotton's relatives. I'll be too busy to think about getting pulled from this case—these cases."

"I'll skip your meeting with Birdie, but I can help with the Whitecottons. I know who some of Gabe's relatives are, and my friend Jed can give me an intro. He's currently on the mainland, going through the Forest Service academy, but he's half-Samish. His mom is from the reservation, and he can grease the wheels for you."

"Perfect. Thanks for helping." She put her hand

to her throbbing head, as she recalled throwing out all her personal details. "As for that other stuff I told you…"

He put a soapy finger against her lips. "Don't worry about it. I believe your side of the story."

Against her will and better judgment, she puckered her lips against his finger. Then she shook her head. "Thank you. I'm not proud of it."

"You don't have to be ashamed of it, either." He whipped the towel from his shoulder and dried his hands. "Do I need to show you the guest room?"

"I think I can find it on my own."

"I'll put a new toothbrush and some toothpaste in the bathroom. Will you need anything else? The sheets on the bed are clean." He held up two fingers Boy Scout-style. "I promise."

"At this point, I'd sleep in my car. I can handle some used sheets." Especially if Tate were the one who'd used them. She could inhale his fresh scent all night like a drug.

Stepping back from his intoxicating presence, she said, "All right, then. I'll see you in the morning. I'm sorry those bones didn't belong to your friend—and I'm sorry they belonged to another boy."

"Me, too."

She escaped upstairs, practically taking the steps two at a time. She ducked into the extra bedroom and kicked off her shoes. Sitting on the edge of the bed, she dug into her purse and found a ponytail holder. She scooped back her hair from her face and took shallow breaths as she listened to Tate come upstairs and open some cupboards. She didn't want to take a chance of running into him in the bathroom.

Finally, she heard the water running, so she crept to the bathroom across the hall. She unwrapped the toothbrush Tate had left for her and brushed her teeth. She washed her face with the liquid hand soap and used a tissue to wipe off the smudge of makeup beneath her eyes.

Blanca tiptoed back to the bedroom and peeled off her clothes. She slid between the sheets and curled on her side, burying her face in the pillow. The clean scent of laundry detergent engulfed her. Tate hadn't been kidding—not that she expected to smell him on these sheets. He was probably fast asleep in the room down the hall.

She rolled onto her back and stared at the ceiling. She'd been nervous about telling him about her past with Manny and the FBI, but he hadn't judged her. She'd been afraid to get too close to him, not wanting to reveal her past to him. But now? Did she have an excuse now? Was she going to allow one mistake to dictate future relationships? That would be giving Manny too much control, and she'd had enough of his dominance in her life.

She flipped back the covers and planted her bare feet on the cold floor. Hugging her naked body, she padded down the hallway to Tate's closed bedroom door. She rested her forehead against the wood, her breath shallow in her chest. She placed her hand on the doorknob and turned.

What the hell was she doing? She stepped back

and released the doorknob. Hadn't she learned her lesson about mixing business and pleasure?

She needed to put Tate Mitchell, the traumatized survivor, ahead of Tate Mitchell, the man she wanted to bed. Or she'd end up with another black mark against her...and her heart broken again.

TATE WOKE UP with a dry mouth, an uncomfortable reminder for why he never drank wine. He hoisted himself up on his elbows and eyed his bedroom door. Had he been dreaming last night when he saw the handle turn?

He'd willed Blanca to enter his room, but his mind games must be on the fritz. Just as he'd been ready to turn back the covers in invitation, she'd fled down the hallway. Probably for the best. She'd had a lot to drink last night, and he liked his women stone-cold sober.

He rolled out of bed and poked his head outside his door. Light from the guest room streamed into the hallway. He cocked his head, on the alert for sounds from downstairs. He thought he'd be up before Blanca, even though it seemed she'd had a hard time getting to sleep, too.

He pulled on a pair of sweats and veered into the spare room. He ran a hand along the fully made-up bed where Blanca's perfume lingered. He then crossed the hall to the bathroom. Droplets of water sparkled in the sink basin, and the toothbrush he'd left for her hung over the edge.

He jogged downstairs, calling her name. A pink

sticky note on the front door caught his attention. She'd ditched him.

He ripped the note from the door and read aloud. "Thanks for the dinner. Wanted to get an early start today. Keep you posted."

With the note stuck to the tip of his finger, he tapped his chin. Blanca had taken a giant leap from almost hitting him up for a booty call last night to hightailing it out of here this morning. Had she heard him snoring?

On his way to the kitchen, he texted her to make sure she'd gotten back to the hotel okay and nobody had broken into her room again.

He stared at his phone's display for a minute and then tossed it on the counter. While he made some eggs and bacon, he kept an eye on his phone. Blanca must've gone straight to work.

Straddling a stool at the counter with his breakfast in front of him, Tate grabbed his phone and left a text for his friend, Jed Swain. In the Forest Service academy, Jed wouldn't have access to his phone until lunch, but Tate laid out why he needed to contact Gabe Whitecotton's people.

He could at least help Blanca with that, even if he couldn't hand her Jeremy's kidnapper.

When Tate got out of the shower, he checked his phone and saw a text from Jed. He'd sent it between classes, but he'd managed to contact Isaiah Whitecotton, Gabe's cousin, and he was okay with meeting with him and Blanca this afternoon.

Blanca still hadn't responded to him, so he called her—harder to ignore that.

She picked up on the third ring, her voice breathy. "Hi, Tate. I was going to text you back from the station. I just came from Mrs. Ruesler's house."

His heart lurched painfully in his chest. "How'd she take it?"

"I guess how you'd think she would. Relieved but tortured at the same time. That's how I'd characterize it." Blanca sniffled. "I obviously did get home okay, and I apologize for sneaking out of there this morning."

Had she snuck out? She must have, as he didn't hear her leave. "No worries. You have a lot on your plate today, and I'm adding more. Made contact with my friend Jed, and he set things up with Gabe's cousin for this afternoon. Does that still work for you?"

"That's great. Thank you." He heard a car door slam and the rev of an engine. "I'm heading for the station right now. Sheriff Hopkins is going to officially reopen Gabe Whitecotton's case. The bones show no cause of death yet, so who knows? Hopkins might try to frame this as another accident, but there's no denying Gabe disappeared as a thirteen-year-old and his fifteen-year-old bones resurfaced."

"The FBI is going to have to send more agents out here, Blanca. Our sheriff's department can't handle this."

"I'm aware of that. Text me a time and location for Gabe's cousin. I also contacted Dr. Summers and left him a message, reminding him we'd met on the search. So I'll need to set something up with him, as well."

"I'll let you know when Isaiah wants to meet."

They ended the call on an awkward note. At least Tate felt the awkwardness. Should he have told her he would've welcomed her into his room and his bed if she'd had the courage to open that door?

He whipped off the towel around his waist and tossed it into the corner. Now, *that* would've been awkward.

LATER THAT AFTERNOON after going through a few reports for work, confirming a meeting time with Isaiah Whitecotton and communicating that time to Blanca, Tate grabbed a jacket from the closet and headed out to his Jeep. He wanted to make a stop before meeting with Blanca and Isaiah.

He drove across the bridge at the falls and made a left turn. Blanca had made a comment the night of the search for Noah Fielding that Tate seemed to make a beeline for that area. He had because it was the same area where he and Jeremy had played, an area not far from the Samish reservation where Gabe had been living at the time of his disappearance.

He parked at the side of the road where small, indistinct trails led into the forest. Taking these trails wouldn't necessarily get you lost. If you knew to follow the river, you could always make it back to the bridge. The same types of trails fanned out from the campsite where the Fieldings had pitched their tent—and lost their son.

Twigs snapped and leaves crackled beneath his hiking boots as he tromped into the woods. Even with winter approaching, the trees closed around him quickly, blocking the weak sunlight. He pumped his legs, one foot after the other, before he could think too clearly about what he intended to do.

He pushed through the underbrush, the bare branches scratching his hands and slapping against his thighs. When he reached the small clearing, he blinked. His gaze locked onto the tree.

With one hand in front of him, he walked toward it as if in a trance. He'd never been back to the tree where his attacker had left him. Closing his eyes, he ran his hand along the bark. What had happened that day?

He and Jeremy were riding their bikes. They'd gotten separated because he'd charged ahead without his friend, but he'd done that many times before. Jeremy was resilient. He never got lost in the woods.

They'd heard the whistling before but had laughed it off. Someone whistling some baby song in the forest didn't scare them.

It should have.

He remembered heading down an incline and then flying through the air as his bike hit something. Is that how he'd gotten the lump on his skull? The doctors didn't seem to think so. The next thing he remembered was someone calling his name and flashlights shining all around him. Jeremy was gone.

He crouched down and scrabbled through the dirt and leaves with his fingers, searching for clues that he'd missed almost twenty years ago. He leaned forward and rested his head against the rough bark of the trunk. It wasn't his fault. He'd been a kid.

The whistling came to him again. This time he knew the tune. The words rasped in his throat. "Put your right foot in…"

His head jerked up, and he choked. He heard the whistle pierce through the trees…and it wasn't his imagination this time. Before he had time to think, his body reacted, fueled by adrenaline and fury.

"Come out, come out, wherever you are. I'm not a kid anymore."

Chapter Twelve

Blanca spied Tate's Jeep on the side of the road, and she hunched over the steering wheel to get a better look. Had his car broken down? Maybe he'd decided to wait for her, so they could enter the reservation together.

She pulled up behind him but couldn't see anyone in the car. She exited the sedan and called his name, cupping her hand around her mouth.

She took a tentative step to the edge of a trail. Even during the day, the forest presented a dark and menacing force. Shaking her head, she barreled ahead on the trail. She was dressed for it today. "Tate?"

A man's shouting seemed to bounce off the trees, coming from everywhere, all at once. She pressed a hand to her galloping heart. "Tate? Is that you?"

More yelling met her question, so she plunged into the forest toward the initial sound. She dropped her gaze to the ground and could tell someone had recently taken this path. Tate had taught her to recognize the signs of flattened grasses and broken twigs on their first search through these woods.

When she got to a small clearing, she caught sight of a blur of blue amid the brown leaves and evergreen needles. Tate had worn that blue jacket before. Why was he running around the woods shouting?

"Tate! It's Blanca. Where are you?"

A figure came crashing through the underbrush, stumbling into the clearing. Tate's wild eyes darted back and forth, the detritus from the forest clinging to his jacket and sticking out of his hair.

"Tate? What's wrong? Are you all right?" He looked like a madman with his head on a swivel.

"Did you hear it? Did you hear him?"

"Hear what? I didn't hear anything or anybody, except you yelling. That was you yelling, wasn't it?" She licked her lips.

Tate dug both hands into his hair, dislodging some of the leaves and dirt. "He was here. I heard him. I wasn't dreaming it this time."

She swallowed. "Dreaming what, Tate?"

"The whistling. I heard the whistling. The same song." He threw his arms out to his sides in a frantic gesture.

Blanca stared past him at the lone tree in the center of the clearing. She put her hand over her mouth. This was it. This was the tree where Tate had been tied up.

She'd meant to come here. It had always been on her task list, but after meeting Tate, she never believed he'd agree to join her.

"A-are you sure?" She glanced over her shoulder, almost expecting to see the whistling man behind her.

"You don't believe me?" His shoulders sagged, and he leaned against that very tree that had changed his life. "I'm sure, Blanca."

"I believe you, but why? Why would he come back to this spot with you here? Why would he want to remind you of what happened?" Did she believe him? It made no sense.

He flapped his arms, as if he intended to take flight. "What does it matter if I remember? I didn't see him. I can't ID him. That's clear, or he would've taken care of me years ago. He couldn't risk my memory returning and my pointing him out on the street. He's not worried about that."

"You think he'd be worried about you catching him whistling alone in the forest? If he is the one who stole the case files from my hotel room, he knows you heard whistling." She pulled at a piece of skin on the side of her thumb, the sting making her regret it immediately.

Tate bent forward and grabbed his knees so suddenly, she thought he was having a medical emergency. She took a step toward him, but he began talking.

"Maybe he didn't even know I was here. Maybe he's out trolling for another victim." He lifted his head as he continued to expel his breath in short spurts. "That's his precursor. His warning. The whistling."

Tate's words triggered something in her brain,

and she gave voice to the thoughts that had floated through her head last night after she'd given up on the idea of seducing Tate.

"He wouldn't take another boy. It's too soon." Pulling up the collar of her jacket to cover her cold neck, she crouched on the ground. She picked up a stick and started stirring the leaves and dirt into a pattern. "Think about the incidents, Tate. Jeremy went missing in 2003, Andrew Finnigan in 2010. If you remembered correctly, Gabe disappeared in 2017, and now Noah Fielding. Notice anything about those years?"

Tate had finally caught his breath. Spreading his legs in a wide stance, he crossed his arms. "Those incidents are all seven years apart."

She nodded, glad he'd picked up her train of thought so quickly. "Seven years between each abduction. Why? What happens every seven years? Is there some event on the island or the bay that occurs every seven years?"

"Not that I can think of." His hands bunched the material of his jacket. "But seven is a notable number, isn't it? There's symbolism to the number seven in the Bible and in other religions, mythology, superstition. It could be anything."

"You're right, and it's his pattern." She tossed aside the stick and dusted her fingers together as she rose to her feet. "Now I'm beginning to wonder what happened in 1996, prior to Jeremy's abduction. Will we find another missing boy?"

"If this has been going on for the past twenty-eight years, we're not looking at a young man."

"Unless we're looking for more than one perpetrator. Maybe it's some kind of satanic cult. I'm sure they'd be interested in the number seven." She clenched her teeth to stop them from chattering. "It's cold, and we have a meeting with Isaiah Whitecotton."

"Right." Tate turned his head to glance over his shoulder at the tree before striding toward her. "Let's get out of here."

When they got back to their vehicles, Tate pointed up the road. "You can follow me, but if I see another car on this road, all bets are off. I'm stopping anyone in the vicinity."

"Got it." Blanca slipped into her car and gripped the steering wheel as she waited for Tate to lead the way. That encounter in the woods, whatever it was, still had him tightly wound. If he'd heard the Whistler for the first time in twenty years, that just might be it. Had he, though?

His Jeep pulled onto the road in front of her, and she pulled in behind him. They'd already passed the sign announcing they were on Samish land, but the reservation lay a few miles ahead. She had her DNA kit and hoped Gabe's cousin would agree to a buccal swab.

When she'd announced at the station today that the remains Tate had stumbled across during the forest fire cleanup belonged to Gabe Whitecotton, missing since 2017, she'd raised more than a few eyebrows and had elicited a venomous look from the usually friendly Sheriff Hopkins. If the bones did belong to Gabe, that news would put another nail in the coffin for Hopkins, even though he had agreed to reopen the case.

Tate made a turn off the main road, and Blanca followed him, passing the wooden sign between two columns of rock welcoming her to the Samish Nation reservation. Small, wooden houses scattered the landscape with mobile homes set farther back from the road. Tate drove past the meeting house in a log cabin, smoke twirling from the two chimneys. A red cross marked the medical clinic in a low-slung building, and Tate crawled past the nation's police station and jail.

After winding toward the edge of the reservation by the tree line, Tate pulled beside a children's playground. A man about their age, a long ponytail hanging down his back, pushed a boy and girl on the swings. When Blanca got out of the car, the kids' squeals made her smile.

Tate waited for her, and they approached the man, Tate's hand raised in greeting. "Hey, Isaiah. It's Tate Mitchell. This is Blanca Lopez with the FBI."

Isaiah ducked around the pumping legs of the children and stuck out his hand. "Good to meet you both. Jed instructed me to play nice, but it's better for me to meet with the FBI out here than in my house with my family around."

Blanca inclined her head. "I get it. Thanks for agreeing to see me."

"If what Tate said on the phone is true, that those bones he found are Gabe's, then there's nothing I'd rather do than to settle this." He stepped back behind the swings and gave each child another push. "Gabe was my little coz, you know? He looked up to me, and I never could figure out why he'd just take off like that without telling me."

Blanca asked, "You didn't think he ran away when he disappeared?"

"I don't know." Isaiah shrugged and tossed his ponytail over his shoulder. "Not like he hadn't done it before. Hell, not like I hadn't done it before. Plenty of young bucks on the rez itching to leave it. You know what I mean? But to leave without saying goodbye…"

He gave the kids another shove, and the girl's little feet reached for the sky.

Had Gabe played on this swing set? It looked old enough. She cleared her throat. "Did your family look for Gabe when he left?"

"All over Discovery Bay. I even went to Seattle."

"Did Gabe have a cell phone?"

"He had a phone. He'd turned it off, and nobody was ever able to trace it." Isaiah had stepped to the side, lost in thought while the arc of the little girl's swing dwindled, and her mouth formed a pout.

"Let me." She stepped behind the swing, pulled back on the rusty chains and let it go with a push. "I'm sorry, Isaiah."

Shoving his hands in his pockets, he asked, "What makes you think those bones are Isaiah's? Aren't you here for a DNA sample?"

"That was me." Tate raised his hand. "When Blanca told me the range of the disappearance and age of the bones, I put it together. Had to be Gabe."

"And you'd know, brother." Isaiah pinched his bottom lip with his calloused fingers. "What is going on? Now this tourist missing from the campsite. You think it's one person, or a series of coincidences?"

"That's what I'm here to figure out." Blanca patted her bag. "Can I get that sample now? It's just a swab inside your mouth. If you think the kids might be scared or bothered by it, Tate can take them to the slide."

"Yeah, yeah. Good idea."

Isaiah grabbed the chains of the boy's swing while Blanca stopped the girl. "Do you want to follow Tate to the slide? Your dad—" she glanced at Isaiah, who nodded "—is going to be right here."

The little boy charged ahead while the girl grabbed Tate's hand and followed.

Blanca covered her smile with one hand.

"He's pretty good with kids." Isaiah jerked his head toward Tate, climbing the steps of the slide.

"His nephew has been living with him recently."

"Right. His sister Astrid's kid."

Blanca clicked her tongue as she unwrapped the buccal swab kit. "These small towns."

By the time she finished with Isaiah and secured his sample in her bag, the kids had abandoned Tate at the slide and were barreling toward their father with demands for hot chocolate.

"Thanks again, Isaiah. I'll keep you posted." She wiggled her fingers at the children. "Bye, kids."

Tate took the bag from her. "I'll carry this for you. When do you think we'll have the results?"

"I'm going to send it to Gwen today. She'll put a rush on it for me. This is getting tangled." She popped her trunk with the key fob, and Tate loaded the bag inside.

"When are you going to lay it all out for your boss?"

"I'm on it." She hugged her purse to her chest. "I'm going to write up something for him tonight and send it off tomorrow, but I'll call first."

"Do you think he'll take you off the case? Add more agents?" Tate scuffed the toe of his hiking boot into the dirt.

"I don't know." She twisted her fingers in front of her. But she had a good idea.

"I mean, you're the one who uncovered links between all these cases. That has to count for something."

"You'd think so." She filled her cheeks with air and puffed it out. "Can I follow you out of here? Not sure I can get back to the bridge in the dark."

Tate tipped his head back, taking in the clouds that were speeding up the darkness of sunset. "At least it's not raining—yet."

Blanca climbed into her car and waited for Tate to make a U-turn back to the entrance of the Samish land. She knew in her gut the same person or group of people were responsible for the kidnapping and perhaps incarceration of these boys. She wanted to see this to the finish line.

As Tate took the curve in the road that would put them on a straight line toward the bridge, Blanca followed his taillights. A light sprinkling of water glistened like diamonds on her windshield, but she didn't know if the rain had come, or they'd entered the area called Misty Hollow by the falls. It seemed too early for Misty Hollow and the bridge.

The red lights in front of her had a hypnotizing effect until they swerved to the side. She slammed on her brakes, and her back wheels fishtailed on the wet road. What the hell was Tate doing?

She cranked up her wipers and squinted through the windshield. Tate had not only stopped his Jeep, but he'd also jumped out of it and had crossed the road into the forest. Had he been hearing whistling again?

She rolled up behind him, her head turned to the side, trying to pick him out across the road. Her palms got damp and her throat dry. She didn't see Tate, but she saw a light, like a flashlight bobbing in the darkness. Was it Tate's? Or did it belong to someone else?

She threw her car into Park and scrambled out the door, catching herself before falling to the road. For the second time that day, she rushed into the forest to find Tate. This time she heard the voices clearly—two men—and she followed the sound through the trees.

A light appeared ahead, and she ran toward it. Her eyes adjusted in time to see Tate take a flying leap at another man and tackle him to the ground.

Chapter Thirteen

Adrenaline pumped through Tate's system as he straddled the man beneath him, his fist drawn back. "What did you do with them? Where's Noah? Answer me."

The man sputtered, his mouth gaping open like a fish on a hook. "Wh-what are you doing? Tate? Tate Mitchell, is that you?"

Tate blinked. The flashlight that had been in the man's hand and now lay on the ground illuminated the area above his head, highlighting curly strands of red hair escaping from a black cap.

Tate ground his teeth together as he drove his knee harder in Porter Monroe's thigh. No wonder he'd been interested enough in the case to show up on the search and approach Blanca. Tate growled. "What did you do with him?"

"With who?" Porter coughed. "Are you talking about the missing kid? I don't know anything about that."

Tate's heartbeat had slowed down to a steady thump in his chest, and then he heard Blanca's voice.

"Tate, what are you doing? Who is that?"

"Porter Monroe. You were right."

Porter gasped. "Right about what? What is this? Let me up so we can discuss this like civilized adults. I don't have any weapons."

"I do." Tate patted down Porter's pockets and waistband. He rolled off him and reached for his gun. He held it on the crumpled form on the ground.

"Can I stand up?" Porter raised his hands. "Don't shoot me. I don't have anything. I haven't done anything."

"You were whistling." Tate ground out the words between his teeth.

"Whoa." Porter staggered to his feet, shooting a glance at Blanca. "Is whistling a crime now?"

Blanca moved to Tate's side, her breath creating puffs of steam in the cold air. "What were you whistling, Porter?"

Porter had gotten to his feet and now jerked his head between Tate and Blanca. "What? What was I whistling? Nothing. I was whistling for my dog, who I'm sure is now even farther in the woods than when I started looking for him."

Tate swallowed. His anxiety receded, making him feel light-headed. "Your dog?"

"What are you and your dog doing out here?" Blanca crossed her arms, bumping her shoulder against Tate's bicep. She had his back.

Pointing at a backpack on the ground, Porter said, "I came back to look for that. It's Zach Snider's backpack. He left it here after a hike. You can ask his parents. They called me to tell me he'd lost his pack, and I told them I'd go back to find it. I brought my dog, Frosty, and he ran off—probably after some critter. I thought he was coming back, too, until you tackled me, Tate. What the hell is going on?"

"Why were you hiking out here with kids?" Tate let his weapon hang at his side, as he took a step to the side and swept up the flashlight from the ground.

Porter narrowed his eyes against the light. "Oh, is that what this is about? A man can't enjoy the company of kids without being a perv? I went through this when Jeremy disappeared, too. Remember that? Of course you do."

"I—we're just trying to figure out what's going on out here." Tate shoved his gun into his pocket. Porter had been whistling for a dog. Had Tate even heard the tune? Had he heard it earlier? Was he losing his mind?

"Look, Porter—" Blanca put her hands out, palms first "—there was some…activity in this area earlier today. You can't blame Tate for suspecting your odd behavior."

"Whistling is odd behavior?" He doffed the cap from his head and used it wipe the sweat from his face. "You can check Zach's backpack, you can call his parents, you can even check on my alibi with Hopkins the day Noah Fielding disappeared—and yeah, he asked me."

"If you don't mind." Blanca walked to the backpack and picked it up. She gestured for Tate to shine the light inside, as she unzipped it.

She examined the typical contents for a kid's backpack. Of course, Porter could've just kidnapped Zach Snider, and then she'd feel foolish. She held out her hand. "Can I see your phone?"

"I should just tell you both to get out of my face, but I'll play along because that's what I always do."

Blanca snapped her fingers. "Enough with the pity party, Monroe. I'm an FBI agent investigating a cold case and current kidnapping. You can't tell me to get out of your face."

He dug his phone from his pocket, unlocked it with his thumbprint and handed it to Blanca.

The blue light of the display illuminated her face as she scrolled through Porter's contacts. She tapped the phone and waited a few seconds.

She said, "This isn't Porter, Mrs. Snider. This is FBI Special Agent Blanca Lopez, and I just have a few questions for you. Was Zach on a hike today with Porter?"

Her gaze darted between Tate and Porter as she said, "Uh-huh...uh-huh. I see... No, everything's fine, and Porter did find the backpack."

She ended the call after a few more pleasantries and held it out to Porter. "Thanks. That clears it right up."

Rolling his eyes, he pocketed his phone. "Is it okay if I keep looking for my dog now?"

"Go right ahead." Blanca waved her hand.

Porter shouted. "Frosty! Frosty!"

He turned to Tate. "I'm gonna whistle now. Is that okay with you, or is that gonna trigger you again?"

"Damn, Porter." Tate wiped a hand across his face. "Go ahead."

Porter let loose with a piercing whistle, which sounded nothing like the "Hokey Pokey" song. Several seconds later a dog barked. Then a white streak materialized, and a snowy white shepherd bounded up to Porter.

Porter pointed to Frosty. "Dog. Can I go now?"

Tate took a deep breath. "Sorry, Porter. It was just—"

"You don't have to explain, Tate. Even though you always try to pretend otherwise, I know you were traumatized by what happened to you. I feel sorry for you, and I feel sorrier for Jeremy."

When Porter stomped off, Frosty trotting at his heels, Tate covered his face with both hands. "God, that was embarrassing."

Blanca rubbed his back. "You don't have to feel embarrassed. Anyone in these woods is suspect at this point, especially if you heard another whistle."

He spread his fingers and peered at her through the spaces. "He was whistling for his dog, Blanca."

"You couldn't know that at the time. Honestly, when I saw that kid's backpack, something pricked the back of my neck." She hunched her shoulders. "The story he told could be true *and* he could be involved in Noah's disappearance. One doesn't necessarily rule out the other."

"You heard him. He has an alibi for the day Noah disappeared."

"So he said."

Tate widened his eyes. "You don't believe him after all that?"

"Let's just say I'm going to check his alibi with Hopkins and look into him a little more closely." She tugged on his jacket. "You're not losing it."

"It sure felt like it."

"Why did you stop your car and get out like that? You didn't hear the whistling from the road."

"I saw his light bobbing in the forest. I had to check it out. Then when I heard the whistle and saw a figure in the dark, all bets were off."

"Just get me out of here. It's giving me the creeps." Her hand slid to his hand, and she laced her fingers with his. "You're *not* losing it, Tate."

He led the way but kept hold of her hand, which seemed to anchor him in more ways than one. "Porter said everyone knew I was traumatized. That guts me."

"He didn't exactly say that." She squeezed his hand. "He said *he* realized you were—probably because he was part of the scene, maybe because he works with young people. Who knows? Maybe that's why he still works with boys—not because he's a perv but because he wants to help."

"But you're still going to check his alibi."

"Better to be safe than sorry." She looked down at the phone in her hand. "Do you want to get some dinner in town after I drop Isaiah's sample at the station?"

"Sure." He opened her car door for her. "I thought you didn't want to be seen with me."

"I guess it's a little late for that now, especially if the FBI is going to send in more agents. We might not have another chance."

"Then, let's do it. You go to the station, and I'll head to the main drag and grab us a table somewhere and send you the address. Preference?"

She dropped to the seat behind the wheel. "I think it's apparent by now that I'll eat anything."

He felt a little stab in his heart. That married jerk had really done a number on her. He bent forward and placed a kiss on her full lips. "I think it's apparent by now that you're a bold woman who knows what she likes."

As THE CAR door slammed and Tate strode to his Jeep, Blanca put two fingers on her throbbing lips. That was maybe the best first kiss she'd ever had. It hadn't just warmed all her erogenous zones, it had also warmed her heart.

Maybe the event in the woods with Jeremy had traumatized Tate, but it had also taught him kindness and compassion. But he'd probably give up all those fine qualities to be just another guy without that experience in the woods.

She followed Tate over the bridge, and the spray from the falls sprinkled her windshield. A few miles later he stopped at a stop sign and stuck his arm out the window to indicate that she should go right to the station. She waved out her window and took the right, as he turned left to head onto the main drag of the town.

A few miles later on the slick road, she parked in front of the station and pushed through the front door. The desk sergeant was on duty, and the squad cars were in the field, which left the station mostly empty.

She greeted the deputy. "Did I miss anything on the Fielding case while I was out?"

"Nothing. Those poor parents and the little sister. Their vacation is supposed to be over in a few days. How do you go home without your boy?"

"I imagine you don't." She patted her bag. "I did get DNA from Isaiah Whitecotton, though. The more of these cases we can tie together, the more that's going to help the Fieldings."

"I hope you're right about those bones belonging to Gabe. You stirred up a ruckus here with your announcement. If you're wrong, you're going to have some egg on your face."

"I'm not wrong." She bumped the swinging door to the back with her hip. "Tell me something, George. Do you have any satanic cults on the island?"

His pale eyebrows shot up. "You mean like human sacrifice and boiling goats?"

"Human sacrifice?" She ran her hand through her hair. "Doesn't have to be that serious. Maybe just some goth kids or stone circles in the woods. Stuff like that."

"Yeah, there are a few kids like that. Dress all in black. The girls look like they have raccoon eyes."

"Yes, exactly like that. Do you know who the kids are?" She grabbed an overnight bubble pouch to send her sample to the FBI lab.

"Unfortunately, my girlfriend's daughter is one of them." He sat back in his chair and wedged one foot on the desk. "She's not a bad kid, just weird. You don't think they had anything to do with Noah, do you? They weren't even alive for Jeremy's disappearance and were little kids for Gabe's, if that's where you're going with this."

"No, I don't think kids are responsible, but I'd sure like to talk to your girlfriend's daughter about a few things. Just curiosity. She's not in any trouble." She put her hands together. "Please, George. You guys aren't gonna like it when several arrogant FBI agents descend on Dead Falls and start pushing you around."

"I can ask Felicity. That's my girlfriend. If it's okay with her, I'll ask Myra, her daughter. I'm sure Myra would love to tell you all about her Wiccan stuff, or whatever she calls it."

"I really appreciate it, George." She slipped him a piece of paper with her cell phone number. "Give me a call when you get the okay."

Blanca addressed the package to the lab and sent Gwen a message that it would be incoming in the overnight pouch. She waved to George on her way out and checked her phone in the station's small lobby. Tate had sent her a pin to a restaurant called the Bay Grill, and she tapped her display for directions.

Would this be her last dinner with Tate? The clock ticked in her ear. Even if she'd nailed it on all these missing boys being connected, *especially* if she'd been right, the FBI would be sending in a team. She couldn't remain the lone agent on this thing. She only hoped she'd get the credit due for blowing it wide-open.

She had a ten-minute drive ahead of her to decide how she wanted to handle her feelings for Tate—because she definitely had feelings. She peered out the glass door. The sprinkles that had started when she'd followed Tate into the woods had turned into a downpour.

George called to her. "You need to borrow an umbrella? We have extras in the back."

"I'm just running to my car. I'll be okay."

The short jog to her car soaked her hair, causing her curls to spiral out of control. She cranked up the heater and shook out her hair.

The wipers could barely keep up with the water sluicing across the windshield, but she knew the way from the station to the heart of the town. She sat forward in her seat and squinted at the road in front of her. She kept her eyes on the white divider line, inching close to it to avoid the soft shoulder on her right.

She'd forgotten how curvy this road was, which she could navigate with no problem in the daytime with dry conditions. As she approached the next turn, she took her foot off the accelerator. The sedan sped up anyway down the grade, so she pumped the brakes.

The brakes squished beneath the pedal. They must be wet. She tapped the brake pedal again, and the car didn't respond at all. The next curve came up quicker than she had time to slow down, but she couldn't seem to control her steering wheel, which seemed to have a life of its own.

She knew enough not to stomp on the brake, so she eased her foot against the pedal. She felt for some engagement, a flare of panic leaping in her chest when she felt nothing but air. She pressed her foot to the floor, and the car lurched into the next curve, speeding up.

She tried to jerk the steering wheel to the left and felt her mistake immediately as her back wheels fishtailed and then hydroplaned. The car now out of her control, she could only hang onto the useless steering wheel as the car lifted off the road. As if in slow motion, the sedan landed with a bounce.

The last thing Blanca saw before squeezing her eyes closed to brace for impact was the shore of the bay rushing toward her.

Chapter Fourteen

Tate checked the time on his phone for the fourth time. Blanca should've been here by now. Should take about ten minutes from the station, fifteen for a tourist.

Rivulets of water streamed down the window of the restaurant, and Tate traced one with his fingertip. Okay, maybe twenty minutes given this weather.

He toyed with his phone. Should he call her? He shouldn't distract her when she was driving, especially in a downpour. He called the station instead.

The desk sergeant answered promptly. "Dead Falls Sheriff's Department, Deputy Vickers. Can I help you?"

"This is Tate Mitchell. I'm looking for Agent Lopez. She was supposed to drop off something there and meet me in town. Have you seen her?"

"Tate, this is George Vickers. She was here but left about twenty minutes ago. You try calling her?"

"Hey, George. Didn't want to disturb her driving. Just wanted to make sure she left already."

"She did." George coughed. "She probably made

a detour to her hotel, maybe to change clothes. I offered her an umbrella, but she went out to her car without one. She probably got soaked."

"You're probably right. I'll give her a call." Tate ended the call and drummed his fingers on the table. Blanca was an FBI agent. She wouldn't answer the phone if it weren't safe to do so.

"Did you want to order anything to drink besides water?" The waitress stood at the table, her tablet tucked under her arm.

"Not yet." Tate tapped Blanca's name from his contacts. The phone rang until it went to voice mail. Tate didn't bother leaving a message.

He left a couple of bucks on the table for occupying it for twenty minutes and ducked outside into the rain. He flipped up his hood and jogged to his car, a ball of dread forming in his gut. If he'd known the skies were going to open, he would've driven her to and from. Tourists got into accidents all the time on the island, and the road between here and the station posed problems even for the locals.

He took the drive slowly, his high beams sweeping the road. No other cars followed or came toward him. Just behind the station, the road meandered down to a boat dock, but nobody would be taking a boat out tonight.

As he fanned out on one curve, he noticed a glow of light coming from the bottom of the incline near the dock. Maybe someone did have a boat out tonight. He rolled into the next turnout and exited his car. He dashed across the road and peered over the shoulder where the grass had been flattened and deep gouges cut into the mud.

It took a few seconds for his eyes to adjust to the dark to figure out that the light emanated from a car turned sideways, wrapped around a tree but upright. It took him a few more seconds to realize the car belonged to Blanca.

He scrambled down the incline, using his hands to keep him from tumbling. Before he reached the car, he almost tripped over a body, stretched out in his path.

"Blanca!" He crouched beside her and felt for a pulse. It beat strong and sure beneath his fingers, and he released a heavy breath.

He ran his hands along the back of her head and felt a lump next to the smaller one she'd sustained the other night at the hotel. Otherwise, it appeared as if she'd decided to take a nap in the rain on the side of an incline.

"Blanca." He jostled her and dragged the top of her body into his lap to elevate her head. "Wake up."

A boom of thunder reverberated in his chest, and a flash of lightning opened the sky. An onslaught of rain inundated them, striking Blanca's face with large drops. That's all it took.

She groaned and blinked. As her lips moved, her eyelashes fluttered.

"That's right. Come out of it. You're okay." It felt like déjà vu, coaxing her from an unconscious state. But it could've been worse.

Now that he was closer to the car, he could see its smashed front end. Had she been thrown from the car, or had she jumped? Or maybe someone had pulled her from the wreckage before he got here.

He glanced over his shoulder as he pulled the phone from his pocket and called 911. Something told him this was no accident. He made his request for help and hung up.

"Tate?"

He brushed her wet hair back from her forehead. "It's going to be okay. I called 911. What happened?"

"Not sure." Blanca winced as she struggled to sit up. "I lost control of the car. The brakes, the steering wheel. Everything seemed to stop working."

"Did anyone…?" He gulped. "Did you see anyone? Any other cars on the road?"

"No, thank God, or I might've run into someone." She got to her knees, despite his suggestion to her to keep still, and crawled toward her open purse, the contents strewn across the ground. She pulled her phone from the mess.

"It's all right, Blanca. I called emergency services." He clambered after her and gathered her things from the rocky dirt. "This time, you're taking that ambulance."

The sirens drawing closer emphasized his point, and Tate stood up to wave his arms. He'd told the operator where they were, but it was still dark.

Blanca sat back down, holding her purse in her lap, looking lost. This time, she probably had a concussion.

He crouched beside her, rubbing her back. "How did you get out of the car?"

"I—I jumped." She cranked her head to the side and gasped as she took in the state of the sedan. "I thought it might go into the water, but it would've been much worse crashing into that tree. I just… I just closed my eyes and jumped."

"Quick thinking." He glanced at the EMTs making their way down the incline with a stretcher. "Were you able to send off the package?"

"The package?" She rubbed her forehead with one thumb.

"The DNA."

"Yes, yes. I'm going to talk to Myra about witchcraft."

"Okay, okay." As the EMTs trooped down, Tate waved his arm. Even though a million questions crowded his mind, Tate stopped questioning Blanca. She needed medical care more than anything else right now.

When the EMTs reached them, Tate jumped up. "She evacuated from the car before it hit the tree, but she seems confused."

The first EMT, a burly guy Tate recognized from numerous fires, asked, "Any injuries you can see?"

"Bump on the side of her head. Scratches on her face and hands. Not sure what else, but she seems dazed."

"No surprise there. What's her name?" The other EMT dropped his medical bag on the ground.

"Blanca."

The EMT touched the back of Blanca's head. "Looks like you're doing just fine, Blanca. Good thing you jumped from the car. We're going to check you out down here first. Then we're going to put you on the gurney and take you for a little ride. Is that okay?"

Blanca glanced at Tate before answering. "Okay."

While the EMTs checked out Blanca, Tate talked to Deputy Fletcher, who'd been on patrol. "She said she lost control of the car."

Fletcher wiped the rain from his face. "Not hard to do in this weather. She's lucky she got out of that car. Wait, that's the sedan we loaned her?"

"Yeah, good job." Tate pinched the bridge of his nose. He didn't think for one minute that car was defective before Blanca started driving it. George at the desk seemed to think Blanca already put a pouch in the overnight mail basket, so what would be the point of stopping her now? If she died, the FBI would just send more agents. In fact, they were in the process of sending more people now. Taking out Blanca wouldn't stop that. How would the Whistler even know Blanca had taken Isaiah's DNA? Someone at the sheriff's department had loose lips.

Fletcher snapped his fingers in Tate's face. "Mitchell. Is Blanca okay?"

"Yeah, sorry." Tate sluiced his wet hair back from his forehead. "I think she's okay but probably has a concussion."

"She's been through the ringer since coming to the island, hasn't she?" Fletcher shifted from one foot to the other. "You think it's related to your cold case and Noah Fielding's disappearance?"

"Maybe." Tate ran the tip of his finger along the seam of his lips. "Keep it quiet for now. Seems like there's a leak at the department."

"Wouldn't surprise me." He poked Tate's shoulder. "They're taking her up."

Tate strode to Blanca, strapped to the gurney, and took her hand. "You doing okay?"

"I'm fine." She squeezed his hand. "I did get the package into the mail. He didn't stop that."

As the EMTs hoisted the gurney over a pile of rocks, their hands disconnected, but there was no doubt in Tate's mind: they were on the same page.

An hour later, Tate sat beside Blanca's bed in the emergency room. Her color had returned, her eyes looked brighter and her cuts had been dressed.

"Mild concussion. Otherwise, I'm okay."

"Can you tell me about the car?" Tate tucked one wild curl behind her ear.

"It was weird. I thought it was just the brakes, but the steering seemed off, too. And the display lights on the dashboard seemed to be flickering." She smoothed her hand along the white sheet beneath her. "I'd felt it before. I should've done something about it."

"Before? Before, when?"

"After our encounter with Porter, on the drive to the station. Something felt off. I just thought it was the rain."

"That makes more sense. Hard to imagine someone tampering with the car in the parking lot of the sheriff's station."

She picked at one of the bandages on her chin. "Which means someone messed with it while we were in the woods with Porter."

"It could've been Porter. He left before we did. He was mad I made accusations against him."

"Now you're saying random residents of Dead Falls resort to violence over suspicions?"

"I'm saying maybe it's been Porter all along. Just because he was in the area legitimately looking for a kid's backpack and whistling for his dog doesn't automatically clear him."

"He does have an alibi for the time Noah disappeared." Blanca gave up and ripped the bandage from her chin, revealing some red road rash.

"You haven't checked that yet, have you?" He tapped his own chin. "Are you sure you should be tearing off fresh bandages?"

"It's annoying. I'm out of here as soon as the nurse returns with some instructions, anyway."

"I'll take you back to your hotel." He held up his phone. "I let the sheriff's department know that the car needed to be checked out. Deputy Vickers told me they'd do it anyway."

"I guess that's another black mark against me with this department." She held up her finger. "First, I lose their files, and now I destroy one of their cars. They'll be happy to see the others come in."

"What were you saying back there about witch-craft? It might've been the concussion talking."

She snapped her fingers. "It might have been, but remember we talked about the number seven and satanic rituals?"

He nodded.

"Turns out Deputy Vickers's girlfriend has a daughter who's into that stuff. Maybe she can give me some information…or names."

"Myra McKay's a Satanist?" His eyes widened. "Who knew?"

"Not a Satanist, or at least I don't think so. More like a Wiccan."

"Oh, that's much better."

The nurse bustled into the room. "You're good to go, Blanca. If you get nauseous tonight or overly tired, you need to come back. Do you have someone who can keep an eye on you?"

Blanca said *no* and Tate said *yes* at the same time.

The nurse shrugged. "Would be better if you stayed with someone tonight, just to make sure you wake up tomorrow morning."

"That's comforting, Vi." Blanca rolled her eyes and winced. "Ow."

"What did I tell you?" Vi handed Blanca a clipboard. "You can sign yourself out. This guy giving you a ride?"

"I am, *and* I'm going to watch over her tonight. Anything amiss, and I'm taking her to the emergency room."

"Perfect." Vi patted his shoulder. "Listen to this guy. He has your back."

Handing the clipboard to Vi, Blanca murmured, "I know he does."

As Blanca hopped off the bed, Tate slipped a hand beneath her elbow. "Does she need a wheelchair out?"

Blanca punched him. "I do not need a wheelchair. Better get going before he has you committing to an overnight stay and room service, Vi."

Winking, Vi said, "I'm sure this hottie could convince me to do just about anything."

As they walked down the hall, Blanca nudged Tate with her elbow. "You have the ladies of every age swooning."

He rolled his eyes and punched the button for the elevator.

Tate had parked his car close to the emergency exit, and as he walked Blanca outside, he asked if she wanted him to bring the car around.

"Isn't that it there?" She pointed to his Jeep. "I think I can handle it."

He kept hold of her arm, anyway, just because it felt so right. When they were both in the vehicle, he jerked his thumb over his shoulder. "I retrieved the stuff from the trunk of the sedan and put it in the back seat. I'm glad you got rid of that DNA sample. Who knows where it would be right now if you hadn't."

"I know we're thinking the same thing about that accident, but why? Would the Whistler go through all that just to steal that sample? And how'd he know I had it, anyway?"

"It's what I told you before, Blanca. This is how small towns work, even during police investigations. You watch. By tomorrow, everyone and his uncle is going to know Myra McKay is a Wiccan. Vickers tells his girlfriend about the DNA, Felicity tells her sister, the sister tells her friend. Who knows who's overhearing this information?"

"So, the Whistler isn't a recluse." She rubbed her chin next to her injury. "Maybe it *will* get better when the rest of the agents arrive. The FBI is insular to a fault. They're not going to be sharing any information with the local sheriffs. Maybe this is why."

"Have you even gotten that report to your boss, yet?"

"Nope."

As they bypassed the center of town, Blanca put a hand to her stomach. "I'm starving. Why do forces keep conspiring to keep us from eating out?"

"Almost everything is closed, and I'm not taking you out like that." He flicked a hand at her.

She glanced down at the rip in the knee of her jeans and the dirt encrusted on her boots. "You're right. I'm a mess."

"But just right for my place."

"Your place?" She twisted a strand of hair around her finger. "I thought you were going to camp out on my hotel room's sofa again."

"Much better at my place. We didn't finish that lasagna, so you can have some of that. Not sure wine is a good idea in your condition, though."

"The last thing I want is a glass of wine, but food

sounds good. In case you haven't noticed, food always sounds good to me." She snorted.

Tate put a hand on her thigh. "Why do you do that?"

Her head jerked to the side. "Do what?"

"Make remarks about how much you eat or how much you like food."

"Do I?" She glanced down at her fingers twisting in her lap.

"You do."

"Honestly, I guess I say those things before someone else can. You know…before someone tells me I'm eating too much or that I could lose a few pounds."

"Did your so-called mentor say those kinds of things to you?" Tate clenched his teeth.

"I—I suppose he did. Yeah, not a very nice guy."

"A manipulator. Clearly, you're beautiful and sexy and perfect the way you are. Any guy telling you something different is just pulling your chain." Tate huffed out a breath.

"Well, thanks. Let's go scarf down some lasagna and whatever else you have in the fridge."

Tate tipped his head back and laughed. "That's more like it."

When they got to his place, he pulled the food out of the fridge. "Do you want to wash any of those clothes? I'm sure Astrid has a robe you could wear."

Blanca plucked at the hole in her jeans. "I guess I'm trendy now. I'll dump them in the wash tomorrow."

He stuck the food in the microwave. "Do you want something to drink?"

"Diet Coke, if you have it. I feel like I need a little caffeine."

"Astrid drinks it, so we should have some." He ducked back into the fridge and grabbed a lone can from the bottom shelf. "Do you feel drowsy?"

"Not really. Could just use a pick-me-up."

He opened the can with a crack and placed it on the counter. After he washed his hands and grabbed some dishes, the timer went off on the microwave. With a pot holder, he took the dish from the microwave and hacked off half the lasagna. He slid it onto a plate and placed it in front of her.

He curled his arm around his plate. "The rest is mine."

She laughed and dug her fork into her food. "I forgot to tell you. I got a call from Dr. Summers, the former ME. He remembered me from the search, although he said he didn't realize I was FBI at the time. Anyway, he agreed to talk to me about Andrew Finnigan's autopsy and the marks on his wrist."

"That's good. Hopefully, he can shed more light on those marks and why the sheriff's department didn't pursue the matter." He crumpled his napkin in one fist. "I saw the televised appeal the Fieldings did for Noah. Gut-wrenching."

"I know. Nothing else found other than the beanie, and the blood is his. No trace of him." She jabbed her fork into a glob of cheese. "If they let me back into the station tomorrow after wrecking one of their cars, I'm going to look up any cases from about 1996.

That's seven years before Jeremy's disappearance, and on this guy's schedule."

"If he does have a schedule."

"It sure seems like he does." She took a sip of her soda and crinkled her nose against the fizz. "Do you think the Whistler tampered with my car?"

"I think he did, but I'm not sure about his motive. If it was to snag Isaiah's DNA sample, I don't see the point. You'd just go back out and get another. It's just like the files he stole from your hotel room. It didn't stop the investigation."

"Slowed it down." She licked some tomato sauce from her lips. "Or he wants to kill me. It must mean I'm onto something. The Dead Falls Sheriff's Department and even the FBI think I'm flailing in the dark, but if I'm really on the right track, the Whistler knows it. The more he throws in my path, the more he distracts me, the longer it's going to take me to figure him out. Perhaps he's hoping I'll get yanked from the case, and new agents will have to start from scratch with my notes and without my secret weapon."

Tate jabbed the handle of the fork into his chest. "I'm your secret weapon?"

"Of course you are. You've been helpful—and you've saved me twice now."

"You saved me, too…from making an ass of myself with Porter Monroe."

"Unless Porter is involved somehow. Then maybe I stopped you from finding out the truth." Her phone buzzed with a text alert, and she wiped her hands before picking it up. "It's Vickers. His girlfriend and her daughter, Myra, gave me the okay to speak with Myra."

"I hope she can give you some insight into the significance of the seven-year gap—if it is a seven-year gap between the abductions. You're not going to tell her why you're interested, are you?"

"Not the details, anyway. It seems as if there's more than enough leaking going on in this town." She pushed her plate away and finished her soda. "Do you mind if I try to get a little work done on my laptop? At least the car didn't go into the bay and ruin all my possessions. Thanks for retrieving them, by the way."

"I have some work of my own to do." He stood up and stretched, all his muscles on display.

Blanca tore her gaze away and shoved back from the kitchen table, grabbing her empty plate. "I'll clean up."

"No way." He tugged the plate from her hand. "You suffered a concussion on top of a concussion. Find some place comfortable to work, or just go on up to bed and work there. I can grab you some of Astrid's things, so you don't have to go to bed in dirty clothes."

She glanced down at her ripped jeans and sweater with debris still clinging to it and grinned. "Yeah, I'm a mess. If you're sure."

"I'm sure. It's not like I'm not used to it. Astrid cooks, and Olly and I clean up. That's the way it is."

"Your sister is lucky." Blanca picked up her laptop case from the floor by the sofa and hitched it over her shoulder.

As she planted a foot on the first step, Tate called after her. "Let me know if you need anything. That toothbrush you used is still in the bathroom."

She made a quick decision before she could think about it too much. "If it's not too much trouble, can I take a shower? After that tumble down the hill and slogging through the mud, my body is probably as dirty as my clothes."

"Sure. In the hallway next to that bathroom there's a closet with towels. There should be soap and stuff in the shower."

"Thanks, Tate."

She took the steps slowly, all her muscles beginning to scream at her. When she reached the upper level, she snagged a towel from the cupboard and went into the bathroom. She started the water to warm it up and shed her clothing. She peeked into the medicine cabinet and spotted exactly what she'd been looking for. She shook out two ibuprofen and downed them with a handful of water.

She stepped under the warm spray and closed her eyes. She'd never been on a case before where she'd been physically attacked. Was that a sign that she'd made it as an FBI agent or that she'd messed up the assignment? Had Manny ever gotten physically attacked on a case? He'd told enough stories, but he always came out the victor.

What an idiot she'd been not to see through his

puffed-up hubris. Looking back, she'd realized Manny had been trying to get into her pants from day one. First, he'd started by telling her Latinos in the department had to stick together. Then after tooting his own horn to make sure she knew how wonderful he was, he'd offered to mentor her. It had worked. She got a lot of plum assignments from her association with Manny. She didn't realize until the end that other agents had assumed she was sleeping her way into favor.

She turned up the temperature on the water and stood with her back to the spray, letting the hot water pummel her. If she got yanked off this case, she'd prove them right.

She grabbed the towel from the rack and dried off, the ibuprofen already doing its work. Not wanting to cover her clean body with her soiled clothing, she wrapped the towel around herself and tucked her clothes under one arm. She opened the door and peeked into the hallway. Hearing Tate downstairs on the phone, she scurried to the bedroom and shut the door behind her.

She tripped to a stop when she saw a filmy baby-blue nightgown draped across the foot of the bed. She placed her own clothes on top of the dresser and rubbed the material between her fingers. Felt expensive. Astrid would probably kill Tate for loaning it out.

She dropped the towel at her feet and slipped the frothy nightgown over her head. She smoothed her hands over her hips, the soft material lustrous beneath her touch. Baby blue wasn't her color, but the nightgown made her feel like a sexy jungle cat.

Turning back the covers, she slipped between the sheets and pulled her computer into her lap. She had to finish that report to Crandall, and damn it, she could do it in a sexy nightie.

Her eyes felt heavy as she typed until her fingers refused to move across the keyboard. Seconds later, someone hovered over her, taking the laptop.

She jerked awake, and Tate froze, the laptop clutched in his hands. "I'm sorry. You looked uncomfortable. I just came in to check on you."

"I'm fine." Yawning, she twisted her head to check the time on her phone. She bolted upright against the pillows still stuffed behind her back. "I've been out for almost two hours."

He brought his face close to hers. "Widen your eyes a bit. Let me see if your pupils are dilated."

"I think it's just overall exhaustion and not the concussion." But she opened her eyes wide anyway, just to bring him in closer.

With his nose almost touching hers, his eyes shifted back and forth, studying hers. "They look okay. Did your shower help?"

"Helped me feel human, and the nightgown helped me feel—" Heat rushed to her cheeks. She'd been about to tell him she felt sexy. What an obvious, embarrassing line. But right about now, she could use it. She was desperate to make him stay.

His blue eyes shimmered like the bay surrounding

this island. "I guess I'll never know how it made you feel, but it makes you *look* sexy as hell."

He still had one knee on the bed, leaning toward her. She grabbed the lapels of his flannel shirt and urged him closer. With the laptop still between them, clutched against his chest, she kissed his minty mouth.

She whispered, "It's not the nightgown. You make me feel sexy and beautiful."

"Because you are." He guided the laptop to the floor and brushed back her curls from her face. He cupped her chin with one hand and touched his lips to hers.

"I'm not going to break." Curling her arms around his neck, she pulled him onto the bed. "Kiss me hard."

He took her face in his hands and angled his mouth over hers, slipping his tongue between her lips. She drew him in, and their tongues did a sweet tangle.

When he pulled away, she gasped at the loss. She flipped back the covers, and in her best husky voice, said, "Join me."

He rubbed his chin. "Are you sure? You're injured, tired."

"And you're just the medicine I need." She patted the mattress. "Besides, I might be gone tomorrow."

He blinked. "This isn't… I'm not…"

She folded her arms over the low-cut nightgown, searching his face. "Did I read this wrong?"

"Maybe you did." He clasped the back of his neck

with one hand. "I'm not interested in some one-nighter with you. I've had enough of that. I didn't ask you to spend the night to hit-and-run."

His words stung. Is that what he thought she wanted? "I—I don't fancy that, either, Tate, but what choice do we have? The agency might pull me off this case. I might be ordered home tomorrow. I want this with you before that happens. I want to feel what it's like to be with a man who values me, even if it is for one night."

He caressed her face, sending ripples of desire across her flesh. "It could never just be one night for us. I won't allow that."

She dragged his hand to her mouth and pressed a kiss on his palm. "Let's see where it leads us."

Already barefoot, Tate pulled off his jeans quickly, as if worried his brain might veto his heart. Blanca unbuttoned his shirt, and he shrugged it off.

Running her fingers along the warm skin of his chiseled chest, she said, "You wear too many clothes on this island."

"It adds to the mystery." He slid his hands beneath the filmy nightgown and skimmed them over her hips. "You feel as good as you look. And I'm sure you taste as good as you feel."

He pulled up the nightie and planted a row of kisses between her breasts and down her stomach as she wriggled beneath his attentions.

When he buried his head between her thighs, she curled her fingers into his shoulders to keep herself from floating off the bed. He brought her to climax, and as her body melted, she knew once would never be enough with this man. She'd need him over and over.

Chapter Fifteen

The following day, Tate scrambled out of bed before Blanca. If he stayed under the covers with her any longer, neither one of them would be able to leave. Even if this did end up being a one-night stand and Blanca took off today, it would be a night he'd never forget. He couldn't regret that.

By the time Blanca made it downstairs, Tate had showered, dressed and made coffee. She entered the room in the same clothes she'd worn yesterday, her hair scooped back in a ponytail, her face fresh and free of makeup.

She glanced at him from beneath her long lashes. "That was quite a night. Thank you."

"You don't have to thank me. You didn't exactly twist my arm." He raised the coffee pot in her direction, and she nodded.

"I know that, but you did have some reservations."

"The second my hand touched your skin I couldn't remember one of them."

"I do have reservations." She hopped up on a stool

at the island. "I have a lot of work ahead of me today, and all I can think about is you."

"I can solve that. I'm off today." He set a mug of coffee in front of her along with some milk and sugar. "I can help you out. Myra? You're in luck. I know her mother. Dr. Summers? I sort of know him, too, although my mom knew him better. In fact, they both might be more open to talking with you if I'm by your side."

"You'd do that?" She glanced at her phone, cupped in her hand. "I'm meeting Myra at about noonish. Just enough time for me to get cleaned up back at my hotel and find out what Hopkins wants to do about loaning me another car."

He tapped his head. "How are you feeling?"

"Fine, except for some sore muscles." She quirked her eyebrows up and down. "But I don't know if those are from the car wreck or those hijinks from last night."

"Hijinks?"

She grinned and sipped her coffee. "Anyway, I could use an ibuprofen, if you have some."

He opened a cupboard where Astrid kept an array of vitamins and snatched a bottle of Advil from the shelf. He shook it before handing it to Blanca. "Knock yourself out."

Her cell phone rang, and she stared at it a second. "It's the sheriff's department. Hope the agency hasn't given me my marching orders."

She picked up the phone, and Tate left the room. If she were getting yanked off the case, he didn't want to be there to witness it.

Minutes later, he peeked into the kitchen. "Good news?"

"Not sure if it's good or bad. That was Sheriff Hopkins. He told me it looked as if someone had tampered with the electrical system in the sedan. So the crash last night was no accident."

Folding his arms, Tate wedged a shoulder against the wall. "That's good news *and* bad news. Good that our instincts were right, and bad that someone is definitely trying to get rid of you."

LATER THAT MORNING, Blanca parked her new loaner in front of his cabin for their meeting with Myra. He'd decided that he should play chauffeur for her around the island.

She walked across his driveway with a stiff gait, and he helped her into his Jeep. He knew that wasn't his fault. When he got behind the wheel, he asked, "Did you take more painkillers?"

"Just before I drove over here. They'll start taking effect soon." She smoothed back her hair, which she'd washed and styled to tone down her curls. "I didn't get a chance to check the database at the station for crimes against children in 1996, but Amanda gave me a token to use to log-in from my laptop. I'm going to want to look into that, especially if Myra confirms our seven-year theory."

"No news on Noah Fielding?"

"Nope."

He shot a sideways glance at her tight expression, as he pulled away from his place. "What's wrong?"

"I talked to my boss this morning, and he's sending in two more agents to look at the Fielding case. He thinks I'm spending too much time on the cold cases, even though technically that's why he sent me out here." She held up her hand as he opened his mouth. "He assured me it's not because he doesn't believe in my investigation. In fact, he was on board with everything I told him about the Ruesler, Finnigan, and Whitecotton cases. He's not convinced Noah's disappearance is linked…but I am."

He released a slow breath so she wouldn't notice. "That's a good thing, right? It doesn't sound like the other agents are going to drive you off."

"No, it doesn't. They'll be here in a few days, so I'm going to try to talk to the Fieldings again before the others arrive."

"You're meeting Myra at her house?"

"Yes, I got the feeling she didn't want Mom listening in, but I'll have to let her if she wants to."

Tate patted his chest. "That's why you have me. Felicity will feel more comfortable letting you talk to Myra with me there."

"Okay, I'll take your word for it." She took her phone from the side pocket of her purse. "Do you know the way? I have directions."

"I know my way all over this island, as long as she's still in the same place."

Blanca tapped her phone. "Riverbend Way. Does that sound right?"

"It does. I know exactly where she is." As Tate

navigated their way to Felicity's house, Blanca hunched over her phone going through emails.

She finally looked up when he pulled into a housing tract with well-ordered homes, emerald green lawns and paved driveways. She blinked. "This is where the Wiccan lives?"

"Seventeen-year-old Wiccan. I doubt Felicity dabbles in the occult." He parked in front of a neat house with garden gnomes stationed in the flower bed. "Although, I don't know. Those little guys look creepy."

"Oh, look, a welcoming committee." She nodded her head at the windshield.

Myra, her black hair loose and hanging over her shoulders sat on the porch next to a young man, about Myra's age, with similar black locks and a sullen expression. "I think we found the Satanists."

"Stop calling them that." She poked his thigh with two fingers. "I think it's just witchcraft, not devil-worship."

"The intricacies obviously escaped me. I'll let you handle the conversation. I'll just stand guard in case they unleash the demons, or whatever."

She clicked her tongue before grabbing the handle of the door. "You're not going to be any help at all."

He followed her out of the car, and she raised her hand. "Hi, Myra? I'm Blanca."

The screen door swung open behind the teens on the porch, and Felicity McKay stepped outside, one hand on her hip. "Oh, hey, Tate. The kids aren't in any trouble, are they?"

Blanca tactfully allowed him to answer.

"Not at all. This is Blanca Lopez. She just has a few questions for…er, them. No wrong or bad answers, just information-gathering."

Felicity circumvented Myra and her friend, hand outstretched, a worried look on her fine-boned face. "Nice to meet you, Blanca. I don't have a problem with you questioning the kids, as long as this isn't anything official. They're just going through a phase."

"Mom." Myra rolled her eyes. "This is Jimmy Cervantes, by the way. He can help. He knows way more than me."

Blanca shook Felicity's hand and then nodded to Jimmy. "Good. Do you want to talk out here?"

Myra stood up, stomping her black Doc Marten boots. "You can go inside, Mom. We'll be okay out here."

"Tate, will you be here, too?" Felicity wound a strand of sandy blond hair around her finger, and he was pretty sure that had been the color of Myra's hair before the severe dye job.

"As long as that's okay with Myra and Jimmy. Blanca's fine with it."

"Let me know if you want coffee or anything. I'll make myself scarce." Felicity squeezed through the two teenagers on the porch and shut the door behind her.

Myra stretched and threw an arm at the chairs on the porch. "Do you wanna sit down?"

"Sure." Blanca climbed the two steps to the porch and claimed one of three chairs.

Tate waited until Myra sat in the other one and then looked at Jimmy. "You want the other chair?"

"Go for it." Jimmy shifted his skinny body, resting his back against the wood column to face the three chairs.

Tate took the last chair. He was finished talking for now. He'd done his part.

Blanca put her hands on her knees. "As you probably know, I'm here on Dead Falls Island to investigate the disappearance of Jeremy Ruesler about twenty years ago."

"Before our time." Jimmy smirked and stretched his legs across the steps.

Tate hoped like hell his sister and her kid weren't still living with him when Olly hit this stage.

"I realize that." Blanca pursed her lips. "But we're seeing some connections between Jeremy's disappearance and a few others on the island, and the number seven keeps coming up in weird ways."

Myra and Jimmy exchanged looks between their black-lined eyes.

"It occurred to me—" Blanca's gaze pinged between the two teens "—that seven is an important number in the occult, and it might have some significance to this case. When I mentioned that to your mom's boyfriend, George, he told me you might be able to help."

"Seven." Jimmy ran a hand through his greasy hair. "It's not just witchcraft and the occult, is it? Seven is important to a lot of religions, including Christianity, the seven deadly sins and all that. But for folklore, the seventh son of the seventh son possessed magical abilities. You get seven years of bad luck when you break a mirror."

"I always wondered about that." Blanca sat forward in her chair. "Why seven years?"

"Oh, oh!" Myra raised her hand, as if they were in class. "The Romans or someone believed that the human soul was renewed every seven years. So if you had seven years of bad luck, you could recover after the seven years."

Jimmy sat up straighter, pulling back his shoulders. "Seven levels of consciousness. The seven sacraments in Catholicism and the seven pillars in Islam."

"Don't forget tarot cards." Myra snapped her fingers with their black-tipped nails. "The sevens are for challenges, but good challenges. A chance to use creativity to solve a problem."

"Wow." Blanca reclined in her chair and clapped a few times. "You two know a lot. So seven might mean renewal instead of death or the end of something. Instead of the end, a beginning."

"Seven is a lucky number." Jimmy cracked his knuckles. "So maybe this guy is using sevens because he feels lucky."

"But why would he kill them?" Myra tilted her head. "For death, he'd use a different number, like thirteen or…"

"Or 666." Jimmy made a gargoyle face and grabbed Myra's ankle.

Tate quashed the smile tugging at his lips. Felicity

had been right. Despite their goth appearance, these two were playing at being different.

Blanca said, "Maybe he's kidnapping them for a different reason. Do you two know of any occult groups or Satanists that might be involved in something serious like this?"

"In Discovery Bay?" Myra snorted. "The most dangerous people I know are the drug dealers. They do a lot worse than we do with our ceremonies in the woods."

Jimmy nudged Myra's foot and ran a finger across his throat.

Blanca flicked her fingers in the air. "Oh, I don't care about your rituals in the woods, as long as you're not killing animals or hurting anyone—including yourselves."

Tate cleared his throat. "And as long as you're not starting fires. Those can get out of hand faster than you might think."

Jimmy avoided his eyes, which told him everything he needed to know. Damned kids.

"Honestly?" Myra made a cross over her heart. "We mostly go out there to try to scare each other... and listen for the Whistler."

Tate's head shot up. "What did you say?"

"The Whistler. You know." Jimmy put his lips together and started whistling a tune that made the hair on the back of Tate's neck stand up.

Chapter Sixteen

Blanca's mouth dropped open. How the hell had these two known about the Whistler? He hadn't even been on the Dead Falls sheriffs' radar. She shot a look at Tate, whose face had blanched.

"Who's this Whistler?" Blanca kept her tone even and clamped down on her bouncing leg by gripping her knee.

Both teens gave identical shrugs. Myra said, "What do you call them? Urban legends? Except this isn't urban. It's a forest legend."

Blanca licked her lips. "What's the urban legend?"

"It's more for little kids." Jimmy chewed on one fingernail, painted black like Myra's. "Something like, *Listen for the Whistler or you'll get snatched.*"

"And he's supposed to whistle that 'Hokey Pokey' song?" Tate finally spoke up, his voice sounding rusty as if he hadn't used it in years.

"Yeah, but slow…and creepy." Jimmy clapped his hands, and all of them jumped. "When you hear that creepy-ass 'Hokey Pokey' song, you'd better run."

He and Myra laughed while Blanca tried a weak smile.

Blanca asked, "Do all the kids know this story?"

Jimmy lifted his bony shoulders. "I guess. We didn't make it up."

Tate jumped up from his chair and hovered over Jimmy. "Where did it originate? Where did it come from?"

Jimmy craned his head back to look at Tate, his lazy dark eyes popping open, his Adam's apple in his skinny neck bulging.

Blanca reached forward and grabbed Tate's hand. "Give him a chance to finish, Tate."

Tate backed off and dropped into his chair, as Jimmy eyed him from beneath a lock of dark, shaggy hair.

"I don't know where it came from. It's like any scary story. It's just there. Just like you don't go to that burned-out barn in Misty Hollow."

"I know I wouldn't." Blanca stretched her lips in an attempt at a smile. "Have any of your friends ever claimed to hear the Whistler?"

"I heard him one night." Myra lifted her chin with a side glance at Jimmy. "Nobody believes me, but I did hear someone whistling that song about a week ago. Freaked me out."

"A week ago?" Blanca counted back the days to Noah's disappearance. "You mean before that tourist boy went missing."

Myra's eyes widened. "Yeah, about then. And it

was right in that general area. I was shook, so I took off running."

"Did you tell anyone about it?" The tone of Tate's voice had returned to normal, and his face had regained its color.

Jimmy thumped his chest. "She told me about it."

"Yeah, and you didn't believe me." Myra kicked Jimmy's boot.

"Why didn't you tell the police?" Blanca asked.

The two teenagers burst out laughing with Jimmy recovering first. "We're not gonna tell the po-po nothing. They don't believe us, anyway."

Blanca wasn't going to be the one to point out to them they'd been talking to law enforcement for the past fifteen minutes. She raised her eyebrows at Myra. "Even George?"

"George is okay, but I'm not going to get involved in anything. Doing this—" Myra circled her finger in the air "—was just a favor to him because he's gonna help me buy a car."

"All right." Blanca rose to her feet and pulled her jacket closed. Dark clouds had started scudding across the sky and rain looked imminent. You didn't have to be a local to figure that out. "I appreciate your help, Myra, Jimmy."

"That's it? You're not going to arrest us?" Jimmy twisted up the side of his mouth.

"I told your mom it was nothing like that, and it isn't. Just some questions, and you were really helpful. You know a lot about that stuff. You're a smart kid. I hope you apply yourself at school." Blanca zipped up her jacket as the first drop of rain hit the steps of the porch.

Felicity poked her head outside. "Do you want to come in? It's starting to rain."

Tate answered. "We're done, Felicity. Myra and Jimmy were a big help. Thanks."

"Oh." Felicity wrung her hands in front of her, as if she were expecting an arrest, too. "I'm glad. You two, get inside, and if you're going into Myra's bedroom, leave the door open."

Myra covered her face with one hand. "Mom."

They all said their goodbyes, and Tate and Blanca ran, hunched over, to his Jeep. They sat in silence for a few seconds while he started the engine and cranked up the windshield wipers.

Blanca flipped back her hood, sprinkling drops of water onto the dashboard. "So all the kids on the island knew about this character, the Whistler, and none of the adults had a clue?"

"I never heard about him. Olly's too young to be part of that crowd. Something to look forward to. It's strange." Tate adjusted his rearview mirror and pulled away from the curb. "That got out somehow."

"And Myra heard him around the time Noah went missing, or just before. What are the odds?"

"The odds are someone's terrorizing the kids of Dead Falls and has been doing it for the past twenty years—and the adults and law enforcement have been in the dark." Tate waved to someone, as they left the subdivision and accelerated onto the highway. "What did you think about their number seven information?"

"I think if Jimmy puts that much effort into his school subjects, he's going far." The windows inside the Jeep had started fogging, and Blanca drew the number seven into the mist on the glass. "It fits what we've been thinking. The Whistler is not kidnapping kids to kill them. It's some sort of new beginning for him."

"He killed Andrew Finnigan."

"Maybe Andrew escaped." She circled her left wrist with her right fingers. "After being held. Look at Gabe—if those bones do belong to him—missing at twelve, fifteen-year-old bones show up. Where was he for three years?"

"After talking to Myra and Jimmy, we can rule out Satanists, can't we? You would think those two might know something about a group like that."

"Probably." She pulled her phone into her lap and plugged it into the charger Tate had snaking from the console. "But those two are babies. They can try all they want with the black eyeliner and the heavy boots. They're harmless."

"Don't tell Jimmy that." Tate snorted. "He sees himself as some kind of occult forest gangsta."

Blanca laughed. "I could send him to East LA where I grew up, and that muchacho wouldn't last ten minutes in the 'hood."

"News?" He pointed to the phone in her lap.

"Lots of texts and emails." She scrolled through the display with her fingertip. "The most important one to me right now is a firm meeting with Dr. Summers. Should I ask him if you can come along?"

"Yeah. As far as I remember, he lives on the other side of the falls, way past Misty Hollow and the Samish land. You don't want to get stuck driving out there in a rainstorm. Sometimes that riverbed floods and cuts off that area from the rest of the island."

She huffed out a breath as she tapped in the question for Dr. Summers. "And I don't think Sheriff Hopkins is going to trust me with another one of his cars in the wild."

"Nothing more about the sedan? Fingerprints? Witnesses? Special skills?"

Twisting her head to the side, she said, "You mean, did anyone need special skills to disable the electrical systems on that car?"

"Exactly. Porter Monroe is a handy guy."

"I read his alibi, you know." She drummed her fingers on the console, next to her charging phone. "For Noah's disappearance. He was on another island."

"We don't know precisely when Noah disappeared. He could've gotten lost first and then had the misfortune to run into the Whistler, who was out hunting."

Blanca's heart fluttered in her chest. "That's what he does. He gets this seven-year itch, or whatever you want to call it, and hunts for his prey."

"It's beginning to appear that way." He jerked his thumb over his shoulder. "Do you have your laptop in that bag? If so, do you want to do some research into 1996 at my place? Or I can take you back to the station."

"Now that I have the token to get into the DFSD's database, I'd prefer to work at your place instead of going back to the station. I don't get a lot of privacy there to work."

"How's that gonna go when the FBI sends more agents out here?"

"Most likely, Hopkins will turn over that big conference room to us. We'll take it over, put in our own computers and equipment and get all linked up to our resources in DC. That's how we roll." Her phone vibrated on the console, and she grabbed it.

"Dr. Summers okayed your presence but changed the meeting place to a coffeehouse in town instead of his place, so I might not need your chauffeuring services, after all."

Tate asked, "What reason did he give for the switch?"

She read his text again. "Said he's coming in to town for dinner with a friend, anyway, and wants to save me the trouble of hauling out to his place."

"If he means later this afternoon, I'll still join you. Maybe we can finally have dinner out ourselves." He cranked his wipers up further as the rain pelted the car.

A little shiver zigzagged down Blanca's back. She was glad she wasn't driving in this mess. She'd take snow with a good set of chains any day. "He wants to meet at four thirty. Is that good for you?"

"I told you." Tate turned his head and winked. "I'm all yours today."

Her mouth watered. "Don't tempt me, or I'll never get any work done."

He pulled into the driveway in front of his house, and they clambered out of the car in the downpour. They stood in the foyer, dripping wet, shrugging off their jackets and leaving their boots by the door.

"Lunch? Soup?" Tate brushed back his damp hair.

"I'm good. I ate before I came over, but you go ahead." She patted the cushion of a sofa positioned in front of the big stone fireplace. "Okay if I set up shop here?"

"Make yourself comfortable. Would you like something to drink?" He crossed the hallway and retrieved a pair of work boots and a slicker. "I'm going outside for a while to make sure things are secure in case this storm gets worse."

"Do what you have to do. You don't have to…entertain me. I'll make myself some tea later."

When the front door slammed behind Tate, Blanca settled on the sofa, her computer in her lap and a pad of paper next to her. She accessed the DFSD's database using the instructions Amanda had given her and did a search on 1996.

A quick scroll-through showed no child abductions or disappearances during that year. She even accessed the years 1995 and 1997. Sighing, she slumped against the cushion. There went her seven-year-itch theory, unless the crime against Jeremy and Tate had been his first rodeo.

She shifted the computer from her lap, stood up and stretched. She strolled into the kitchen and made herself a cup of tea. As she dredged her tea bag in the hot water, she stared at the steam rising from her mug. She'd checked for kidnappings but hadn't looked at the runaways. Would the database contain runaways if the deputies never considered the incident suspicious?

She dropped the soggy tea bag into the trash and returned to her laptop. She did a search for runaways, but the database wasn't going to make it that easy for her. Unless that word was in the heading, the file wouldn't pop up in the findings. She'd have to dig deeper.

Lost in her research, Blanca jumped when the front door swung open, and Tate stomped his boots. "It's a mess out there."

Putting her hand to her throat, she said, "You scared me."

"Any luck?" After he removed his boots, he hoisted a canvas sack over his shoulder, shedding drops of water on her head as he walked behind the sofa. He placed a sack on the hearth of the fireplace and unloaded several piles of wood. "I'll light a fire later. It's too close to our meetup with Dr. Summers."

"It is?" Her gaze darted to the time in the lower corner of her screen. "That went by quickly."

"Did you find anything?" He stacked the logs in a heavy metal container on the hearth.

"It's slow going." She pinged her fingernail at her screen. "No abductions or missing children from 1995 to 1997, but Andrew Finnigan wasn't listed as missing, and neither was Gabe Whitecotton. So I'm going through again, looking for runaways."

"You should try checking into troubled youths, too. Why did the Whistler start abducting adolescent boys? There had to have been some inciting incident for him, some reason. Maybe some teacher got punished for inappropriate actions with a boy. He saw himself as innocent and then started lashing out."

She tilted her head. "You've got some imagination. Sounds plausible, but I hope you're wrong on that one. The principal of the elementary school on the island killed those two women a few months ago. If the Whistler is a teacher, the parents are going to storm the school board with pitchforks."

"Yeah, but maybe that's what you're looking at. Bryan Lamar, the principal, had a grudge…and he was a psychopath. It may be the same situation here— someone with a score to settle."

"And the seven-year pattern?" She pushed the computer from her lap and rubbed her warm thighs.

Crouching beside the fireplace, Tate clapped his gloved hands together over the pile of wood. "Like the kids said. He's trying for some sort of fresh start or renewal."

"You're good, Tate." She clicked on a tab in the database. "Here are a couple of accidental deaths in 1996. Ugh, a five-year-old drowned, and a toddler choked."

"Can you look at those later? We're going to be late for Dr. Summers. I already missed my window to take a shower, but I can at least change my clothes."

"You—" she kicked off the fuzzy throw blanket from her leg and sauntered toward Tate, placing her hands on his shoulders "—look like a sexy lumberjack."

In one movement, he got to his feet and wrapped one arm around her waist. He planted a chaste kiss on her closed mouth. "Do you want to make us even later?"

Her cell phone rang, and she placed her hands against his chest. "Saved by the bell."

As she grabbed her phone from the coffee table, Tate hovered over her shoulder. "Who is it?"

Glancing at the display, she raised her eyebrows. "It's the FBI lab."

She tapped the screen to answer. "Gwen?"

"I have some news for you on the bones."

"Go ahead. I'm putting you on Speaker." Her eyes met Tate's.

"Your hunch was correct. These bones are a familial match to the DNA you submitted from Isaiah Whitecotton. They most likely belong to a fifteen-year-old Gabe Whitecotton, and they've been in that grave for about four years."

Chapter Seventeen

Blanca chatted with Gwen for a few more minutes, and she assured Blanca she'd email the report to her this afternoon.

She dropped the phone on the sofa. "That's it. Your instinct was correct."

"Which means Gabe was kept captive somewhere before he was murdered. This is going to be rough on Isaiah and the family."

"On all the families." She gave Tate a push. "We need to get going. It's more important than ever to hear Dr. Summers's take on Andrew Finnigan."

Tate bolted upstairs, and Blanca folded the blanket and put her laptop on the coffee table next to her notes. She took her empty mug into the kitchen and rinsed it in the sink, feeling very much at home. Ever since last night, she and Tate had been tiptoeing around, trying to pretend they hadn't thoroughly explored each other in the most intimate way. This afternoon felt more natural.

As she freshened her makeup in the mirror at the foot of the stairs, Tate bounded down the steps wearing a pair of dark jeans and a plaid blue-and-green flannel, hanging loose over a blue T-shirt that matched his eyes.

She smacked her lipsticked mouth in the mirror. "Now you look like a sexy, *clean* lumberjack."

"I'll take that." He pointed to her laptop. "Are you ready?"

"Yes, I'm leaving that there, if it's okay with you. I'm still logged in and want to pick up where I left off. You're not expecting anyone to come into your house, are you?"

"I'll lock up, and I installed a security system a few months back after…an incident with my nephew."

She widened her eyes. "Your nephew's not twelve-years-old, is he?"

"Not yet, and it was nothing like that, but Astrid is a little jumpy."

"I can't say I blame her. Don't get me wrong. The cabin is beautiful, but it's still a little isolated."

"A lot of these places are. We have plenty of un-developed land on Dead Falls. It's one of the least developed islands in Discovery Bay but the most populated because of its size." He grabbed his dried-off jacket by the door. "Are you ready?"

"I am." She patted the jacket she'd left by the front door, and hers had dried, as well. She zipped it up and pulled her gloves from her pocket.

When she stepped onto the porch, she tilted her head back to look at the sky. Despite the solid gray color, the rain had stopped for now. "Do you think the rain will start up again?"

"I'm sure of it."

Tate opened the passenger door for her, and she hopped into the Jeep. When he settled beside her behind the wheel, she said, "We're meeting him at Coffee Time in town."

"That's a popular spot, but it's close to some restaurants where we can grab a bite after meeting with Summers. In fact, it's near the Grill, where we were supposed to have dinner last night."

"Perfect." She adjusted her seat belt, nudging the bag at her feet. "I brought copies of the autopsy report and a few pictures of Andrew's body with some close-ups of his wrists. I hope he remembers after all this time."

"He was on the search with us. He didn't seem infirm or anything. I'm sure he'll have recollection of what he wrote at the time."

Raindrops started hitting the windshield by the time they rolled into town, and Blanca hunched forward in her seat. "Still pretty busy. The rain doesn't seem to stop people from going out."

"We have to adjust, or we wouldn't go anywhere. Plus, it's Christmas in a few weeks. People have things to do and places to go."

She slid him a glance. "Including you. When are you supposed to head out to Florida to see your mom?"

"Scheduled to leave in a little over a week, but I can always change that ticket." He parked the car and poked his head out the door, twisting to look at the sky as a flash of lightning cracked overhead. "Damn, this is bad news for the forest, even in the rain."

Blanca didn't wait for him to get her door. She landed outside the Jeep and flipped up her hood. She'd seen the sign for Coffee Time when they were driving up, so she hunched over and scurried to the sidewalk where the blue-striped awning shed fat drops of water.

Tate caught up to her and got the door.

The scent of coffee blasted Blanca as she stepped inside the warm shop. Even inhaling it made her feel warm inside. She flipped back her hood and shivered.

The spare, gray-haired man in the corner raised his hand, and she nodded in Dr. Summers's direction. Grabbing Tate's sleeve, she said, "He's over there at the corner table. I'm glad he chose a private spot for what I have to show him."

They hung their wet jackets on the pegs by the door, and their feet squelched across the floor to the medical examiner's table.

Blanca stuck out her hand. "We meet again. Thanks for agreeing to see me, Dr. Summers."

"Happy to help." He slipped his bony hand from hers and shoved it toward Tate. "Good to see you again, Tate. How's your mother?"

"Mom?" A crease formed between Tate's eyebrows. "Oh, that's right. You two were friends. She's fine."

Dr. Summers tapped his coffee cup. "I already ordered, trying to stave off the chilly weather. Hope you don't mind."

"Of course not." Blanca settled her purse and bag on the floor, and turned toward the counter.

Tate touched her arm. "I'll order. You have a seat with Dr. Summers. What do you want?"

"Vanilla latte, please."

"I'll be right back."

As Tate made a beeline for the counter, Blanca took the seat to the right of Dr. Summers. "I brought the autopsy report and a few pictures to jog your memory."

"Good. I'm going to need that." He tapped his head. "The brain doesn't work the way it used to."

Blanca nodded, but her gaze took in the doctor's lean but fit form, his close-cropped gray hair emphasizing a pair of high cheekbones and light blue eyes. The man didn't look a day over sixty, hardly old and senile. Why'd he retire so early?

"I always heard it was a good idea to keep exercising your brain as well as your body in retirement, just to stay on your toes."

He slurped a sip of coffee. "I try to run, and I cut my own firewood. I even do a few crossword puzzles."

"Well, I'm going to try to give your brain a workout today." She pulled the bag toward the legs of her chair and unzipped it. She pulled out the file and placed it on the table.

Tate returned with their coffees and took the seat beside Blanca.

Summers leveled a gaze at Tate. "I heard Ingrid moved to Florida. Divorced from your father?"

Tate raised his eyebrows, as Blanca bumped his knee under the table. "Yeah, she's in Florida. My sister and her son are visiting her now, and yes, she and my father are divorced."

"Damn shame." Summers scratched his sharp jaw.

Blanca drummed her fingers on the file folder. "So the autopsy of Andrew Finnigan."

"Accidental death from a fall." Dr. Summers leaned back in his chair, folding his arms. "He could've jumped, but we wanted to spare the family that torture."

"I know that, but I did see something curious in the photos of Andrew's body." Blanca opened the folder and with one finger pulled out a photo. She maneuvered it around so that it faced Dr. Summers, and she tapped Andrew's wrist. "Do you see something there?"

Summers pulled a pair of glasses from his front pocket and perched them on his nose. Even with the glasses on, he squinted through the lenses to study the picture. "No. What am I looking at here?"

Blanca bit down on her frustration and drilled her finger into the photo. "Right there. Red marks on his wrist. You even noted them in your report."

"I did?" He picked up the picture and gave it another look. "Yeah, I see it now. Significance?"

Blanca took a sip of coffee and licked the foam from her lips. She shoved another photo under Dr. Summers's nose. "Now, look at the other wrist."

Again he squinted, bringing the picture close to his face. "I do see that."

"Both of those marks look similar to me. They look like signs of restraints. Zip ties. Rope. They're the same shape and size. Surely, nothing in a natural fall—accidental or on purpose—would cause those marks. You even mentioned them in your report as suspicious."

"If you say so, Blanca." He massaged his temple with two fingers. "As I said, my memory isn't what it was."

She pursed her lips. She got it. Dr. Summers could claim memory loss now so he wouldn't be judged for not pressing the issue. "I have your report here."

Dr. Summers scanned the first page of the report with a slight quirk of his thin lips. "This brings back memories, for sure."

"Do you see what you wrote on the second page regarding the ligature marks?"

"Ligature marks?" His eyebrows practically jumped to his hairline as he turned the page of the report. "I doubt that I characterized these as *ligature marks*."

"Well, you did point them out as suspicious." Blanca jiggled her leg up and down, and Tate clamped a hand on her knee to stop it.

"You're right. I did." He ran his finger across the page. "I remember now. Yes, two red marks on his wrists, similar in size and shape, and no apparent cause for the injury, although a lot can happen in a fall."

Blanca blew out a breath. She finally felt as if she'd pulled the tooth. "You had that in your report, but there was no follow-up."

"That's right." He let the page of the report fall back onto the table. "I remember some kind of discussion with Sheriff Maddox, and the conclusion was accidental death."

"But you had your doubts." Blanca felt like a dog with a bone.

"I did, indeed." He skimmed a hand over his short hair. "Mad Dog Maddox was not someone who brooked disagreement. He wanted the case closed."

Tate cleared his throat. "Are you saying that Sheriff Maddox coerced you into that decision?"

"Coerced." Dr. Summers steepled his long fingers. "I suppose you could say that. He was a very convincing man."

Tate continued, "What about the lack of animal activity on the body, Dr. Summers? I'd always heard rumors about that, too. If Andrew's body had been out there for several days, there should've been more…degradation from animals."

"I do remember that. The boy could've been in the caves." He swirled the dregs of his coffee. "Where are you going with this, Blanca? You think this is tied to this current case with this boy… Jack?"

Blanca corrected him. "Noah."

Summers snapped his fingers. "That's right. Do you think there's a connection?"

Blanca planted her elbow on the table and sank her hand in her palm. "You heard about the bones Tate discovered last week."

"Of course." Summers glanced down. "I heard

that might be Tate's friend gone missing all those years ago."

Shaking her head, Blanca said, "That's just it. Those bones don't belong to Jeremy. They belong to another missing boy. I just got confirmation this afternoon. I have a theory that these boys were being held."

Summers jerked back and grabbed at his hair. "Oh God, no. Whose bones were they?"

"There's a familial match to Gabe Whitecotton."

A furrow formed between Summers's eyebrows. "I don't know that name. Treated some Whitecottons out at the reservation before."

Tate said, "Same family."

"That's a damned shame. I can see why this has piqued your interest, Blanca. I'm sorry I can't offer much more. I did notice those marks, made note of them in my report, as you can see, and was probably bulldozed out of further inquiry by Mad Dog." Summers spread his hands. "You remember how he was, don't you, Tate? Ingrid never liked him."

Blanca kicked Tate's foot. "If the FBI reopened this case, Dr. Summers, would you be available for comment?"

"Absolutely."

They all jumped as thunder rattled the windows of the coffeehouse.

"I have another fifteen minutes or so before my dinner date. I'd be happy to skim through the rest of the report with you, Blanca. Can you give me a minute while I use the men's room?"

"Sure, that would be great." She turned to Tate. "Do we have some time before dinner?"

"Sure. Maybe the weather will settle down."

Summers excused himself from the table, and when he turned the corner to the bathrooms, Blanca laughed. "Does he have a thing for your mom, or what?"

"I know, right?" Tate tugged on his ear. "I kind of remember that. I'll have to ask Mom about him."

"Was he married, too?"

"Not sure. Divorced, I think." Tate put a finger to his lips.

The chair scraped as Dr. Summers took his seat. He rubbed his hands together. "Okay, show me what you got."

Blanca flipped over a few more pages of the report. "Can you look at these findings? I think I know what they mean, but I could use some layman's terms."

Summers hunched over the papers on the table at the same time Tate's phone beeped.

Blanca put her hand to her throat. "What's that? I've never heard your phone do that before."

Tate had grabbed his phone and stabbed at the screen to stop the alarm. "It's a fire. Seems like lightning struck a tree and set it ablaze. The rain hasn't been enough to dampen the fire. Sorry about dinner, Blanca."

"That's all right. Get to work. Dr. Summers and I will finish up here and… Oh."

"Exactly. You don't have your car. You can probably get a rideshare to my place if you call now."

Dr. Summers looked up from his own phone. "Looks like the weather scared off my old pal. I'll take Blanca to her hotel or to your cabin, Tate. It's on my way home."

"If you don't mind, that's perfect." She flicked her fingers at Tate. "Go. I'll be fine."

He leaned in and kissed her on the forehead. "I'll meet you back at my place when I'm done."

When he left, Blanca and Dr. Summers continued reviewing the report, and the doctor really seemed to have changed his mind about the method of Andrew's death.

As she packed the file away, Blanca said, "I'm glad we'll have you on our side, Dr. Summers."

"My pleasure. You can call me Scotty. All my friends do." He pushed his chair back. "Now, do you want a refill, or are you ready to head out?"

"I'm ready. I hope Tate got out to that fire okay and that it's not too bad."

"He's a professional." Scotty pushed to his feet and said, "Oops, you don't want to forget this."

He bent over and picked up her phone from the floor.

She twisted her lips, as she took it from him. "How'd it land on the floor?"

"It was next to your purse."

"Thank you." She tucked the cell phone into the side pocket of her purse where she usually kept it and stood up. "Do you know where Tate's cabin is?"

"He grew up on that property, although the family home wasn't nearly as grand as what he has now.

That whole family came into some money when the grandfather died. I think that's when Tate's parents divorced. Gordo, Tate's father, saw his chance and took off for Costa Rica or someplace like that."

Blanca put her hand over her mouth to hide her smile. Dr. Summers had feigned ignorance about Tate's mother's marital status, but apparently he knew the whole story. Knew more than she did about Tate's family.

They stopped at the door, and Scotty helped her on with her jacket. A steady rain accompanied them to Scotty's truck, parked on the street. He got the door for her.

When he got behind the wheel, he said, "Where to?"

She jerked her head to the side. "Um, Tate's place, right? Is that still okay? I don't want to put you out."

"No, no. That's fine. I just thought you might want to go back to your hotel first."

"My car is at his place. I had a little…accident last night, so he's playing chauffeur." How did Dr. Summers even know where she was staying? He was quite the busybody.

"That's good. Tate matured into a fine man, even though Ingrid had her hands full with him." As he started his truck, his phone blared an alarm.

Blanca jumped. "What is it with the phones out here? Doesn't anyone have a normal ring?"

"I have alerts from the DFSD." He cupped his phone in both hands. "Oh my God. There's been a sighting in the woods of Noah Fielding. They're calling on people to fan out and search. I… Is it okay if I just drop you off at your hotel? You can take a car to Tate's, like he said. I'm really sorry."

"No, no." Blanca snapped her seat belt. "I'm in. Let's go."

Scotty's truck lurched forward on the slick street. "I was hoping you'd say that, Blanca."

Chapter Eighteen

Tate tossed some gear in the back of the Forest Service truck, rivulets of water trailing down his uniform.

His second-in-command, James, swore beside him. "I was just getting ready to sit in front of the fire with my woman and a bottle of whiskey."

Tate smacked him on the back. "At least it wasn't serious."

Aaron joined them, piling more equipment in the truck. "I don't know about that, Tate. Someone purposely set this fire. That's pretty serious."

Tate shrugged. "Maybe some teens thought it wouldn't be a problem to set a fire in a rainstorm. Anyway, it all ended okay."

James shoved him. "Tate's anxious to get back to his FBI agent."

"And for that—" Tate slammed the keys against James's chest "—you're taking the truck back to the station, and I'll be in front of my fireplace before you will."

At the time of the alarm, Tate had gotten instructions to head to the site in his own vehicle, as others were coming from the station with the trucks. He'd been annoyed at the time, but now he was happy to have his Jeep to get back to his place…and Blanca. She should be there by now.

He punched on the ignition and let his Jeep idle and heat up as he texted Blanca. He stared at his message on the display, frozen in place. It hadn't been delivered. Could be his location. He flicked his lights at the boys, as he rolled away from the fire site.

His four-wheel drive gripped the road as he wound back to his cabin. He parked behind Blanca's DFSD sedan and jogged to his front door. He disabled the security system with his phone and slipped his key into the lock. A fire in the fireplace sounded good about now.

As he slammed the door behind him, he called out for Blanca. "You get here okay?"

The silence came back at him in waves, and he felt a prickle at the nape of his neck. He flicked on the lights of the empty kitchen. He'd figured she might've picked up some food or at least opened a bottle of wine.

He pulled out his phone, and his heart did a double thump when he saw his previous text message to Blanca still frozen in place. It had never gone through. He tapped the phone to call her and it went straight to voice mail.

"Blanca!" He took the stairs two at a time and veered into the empty spare room, the bed made and the nightgown he'd loaned to Blanca across the foot, just as they'd left things this morning.

He went back downstairs and sat on the sofa she'd occupied earlier. Maybe Summers had taken her back to her hotel and she'd decided to stay there. He called the hotel and discovered she hadn't been there all day. The clerk rang her room just in case but didn't have any more luck than Tate.

If she thought he'd be working all night, she might have gone to the station to follow up on something. Her laptop was still here, though. He called the DFSD station anyway, and the desk sergeant told him Blanca hadn't been in since the morning to pick up the new car.

Could she and Summers have decided to have dinner together? That seemed weird, but they'd appeared to be hitting it off when he left the coffeehouse.

He did a search on his phone but couldn't find a number for Dr. Scott Summers. The station might have it from the search the other night. The deputies had asked the volunteers to leave their phone numbers if they wanted to be alerted to new searches.

He called the sergeant back at the station, but he wouldn't release Summers's phone number to him.

He flipped open Blanca's laptop. She'd stayed logged in, so he was able to bring up a search engine. He did a search for Summers but found only out-of-date info about his practice.

He snorted. Maybe his mother had his personal number. The man's interest in Tate's mother was strange. Did she know Dr. Summers harbored some secret crush on her?

Maybe Blanca and Dr. Summers were having dinner together and Blanca's phone was dead or the storm had messed up her service.

He chewed on the inside of his cheek and navigated back to the DFSD database Blanca had been searching. She'd left the page up with the two incidents involving children from 1996.

He clicked on the first one. A five-year-old boy had drowned at a birthday party by a creek. As he skimmed the report, a name jumped out at him: Summers. Jackson Summers. Tate trailed his finger down the screen.

Jackson Summers was the son of Lydia and Dr. Scott Summers. He'd fallen into the rushing creek while the children were dancing to the "Hokey Pokey" song.

BLANCA PANTED AS she clumped after Scotty. "Hold up a minute. Are you sure you have the right location? I don't see any other searchers here."

"This is what they told me." Scotty stopped in the clearing and spread his arms out to his sides. "It always ends up being here."

Blanca had bent forward, hands on her knees to catch her breath. As she straightened up, her eyes widened. This was the place—the tree where Jeremy's abductor had left Tate.

"They told you to come here? Do you know what this place is?"

Scotty ran his hand over the trunk of the tree. "I do. Tate Mitchell was found here, tied up, blood in his shoes."

Blanca cocked her head. Did everyone know about the blood in Tate's shoes? "And the alert said to meet here? Was Noah seen here? Did he run away?"

Shoving his hands in his pockets, Scotty said, "Noah's safe, and he'll stay safe as long as you keep your nose out of our business."

Blanca massaged her fingers against the lump on the back of her head, which had started throbbing. "Wait. He's safe now? They found him?"

"He's safe with me. He's mine now."

The world tilted, and Blanca took a step to the side to regain her balance. "Wh-what are you talking about, Scotty?"

"I'm talking about my son." Scotty took a gun from his pocket and aimed it at her.

Her knees weakened, and she felt for her purse with her gun inside, which she'd left in Scotty's truck. She traced the edges of her phone in her pocket but already knew it would do her no good. She'd tried using it in the truck with Scotty, but it had been dead. He'd done something to it in the coffeehouse to make sure she wouldn't wonder why she hadn't received any alert about a search.

She choked. "The fire calling Tate away?"

"I set that fire on slow burn and phoned in the report when I was in the bathroom." He caressed the bark of the tree. "I knew Tate would go. He's a solid man now, but he wasn't always that way. He was trouble, unlike Jeremy. I knew I could handle Jeremy, but Tate would be a handful. Also, I didn't need two sons. Just one to replace the one I lost."

Blanca drove a fist against her mouth, and her lips cut the inside of her lip. "Where is Jeremy? What did you do with him?"

"I kept him with me. I kept him safe and raised him as my own."

"Is he alive now? Where is he?" She scanned the ground for a rock or stick she could use as a weapon. Against a gun?

"He got too old, didn't he? You raise a son and then set him free."

"The same way you set Andrew Finnigan and Gabe Whitecotton free?"

"Andrew was too much trouble. I should've known that. He escaped…and had an unfortunate fall. Gabe—" Summers practically beamed and puffed out his chest "—Gabe was a good son, but teenagers are hard to handle. If you ever have kids…"

Blanca gulped. She wanted kids right now more than anything in the world. She wanted a life. "Where is Noah, Scotty? Just tell me where he is. I'll let you leave. You can take off. Just give us Noah."

Summers chortled, an eerie sound out here in the woods, more animal than human. "You'll let *me* leave. That's rich, Blanca. I'm the one with the gun. Yours is in my car, and I slipped the battery out of your phone when I took it with me to the men's room."

"You can kill me. It won't matter. I'm part of the Federal Bureau of Investigation. Agents will keep coming and keep coming until they find Noah and figure out what you did. When I disappear, they'll take over the investigation of the other two attempts you made on my life—at the hotel and the car. That was you, wasn't it?"

"Those weren't attempts on your life, Blanca. I wanted to put a little scare into you and get my hands on that case file at the same time. I have to admit, I rigged the car in the hope that you'd crash and get injured enough to get off the island. These other FBI agents you talk about won't be nearly as dedicated as you." He gave her an exaggerated wink that turned her stomach. "You have a personal stake in this now, don't you?"

She dug the heels of her boots into the mulch on the soggy ground. "Tate saved me both of those times, and he'll figure it out in the end."

He kicked the bottom of the tree. "You have such faith in Tate. Why? He couldn't save his friend, Jeremy, and he can't save you. He's off fighting a fire somewhere. He's not going to have any reason to think I killed you. Why would he? Why would anyone? I've been hiding in plain sight all these years, joining searches, performing autopsies. And I have my little family safe at home."

"Why are you doing this, Scotty? If you wanted a family of your own, you could have adopted a child." She suppressed a shiver at the idea of this man adopting.

He hissed between his teeth. "I had a child. A son. He drowned when he was five, playing a game at a birthday party, too close to the creek. I was working. It was my wife's fault. They never should've been there. So seven years after his death when he would've been twelve years old, I took another twelve-year-old boy to keep as my own."

"And seven years after Jeremy, you took Andrew, but that didn't last." She pressed a hand to her heart. "Why seven years?"

"Seven years is a time for renewal, for rebirth. Every seven years, I give myself a new son to replace Jackson."

"I'm so sorry for your loss, Scotty, but this isn't the way. You know the grief of losing a child. How can you take someone else's child from them? What about Birdie Ruesler? What about the Fieldings? How can you send them home without Noah?" The only thing that kept her hopeful was the belief that Noah was still alive somewhere. Was that why Scotty didn't want her to come to his place? He had Noah there?

He puffed out a breath from between his lips. "I never felt bad for Birdie. Her son was alive. Noah will be fine, too."

"Before…before you kill me, can you show me? Can you show me where Noah is and that's he's okay?"

"Oh, Blanca. You're just going to have to take my word for it. You're going to die right here, and poor Tate will have even more reason to avoid this part of the forest."

Chapter Nineteen

Tate navigated his Jeep through the road cutting through Misty Hollow. The rain pounded the hood of his car, and the windshield wipers kept his thoughts on track. *Find Blanca. Find Blanca.*

As he approached the road to Scott Summers's sprawling property beyond Misty Hollow, he cut his lights. Would Summers have some kind of security system? Booby trap?

He parked behind a copse of trees and slid from his car. He crouched low, his gaze pinned to the main house, low lights beaming from the windows. When he didn't see Summers's truck, he almost collapsed to his knees.

He crept to the house and peered into the windows. Through a few gaps in the drapes, he spied the rooms of Scotty's house: neat, nobody there.

He continued to slog through the mud into Summers's backyard. A few outbuildings dotted the property—dark, windowless structures that looked ready to fall over.

He rounded the corner of one and tripped to a

stop. A building on the edge of the property had seen some improvements. As Tate stared at the structure, he noticed a glow of light emanating from the back.

He took out his gun and circled the building. The door had a padlock on the outside, and he grabbed a shovel and pounded the lock until it broke and fell to the ground. He kicked in the door, gun leveled in front of his body.

Someone yelped from the back of the building where he'd seen the light, and he crept forward. When he got to the end of the space, another door met him. This one opened to his touch.

It creaked as it swung open, and Tate held his breath. He sputtered as his gaze landed on a large cage, a dark-haired boy clinging to the bars with both hands.

Tate's heart pounded. "Noah Fielding?"

The boy's hands tightened on the bars. "Who are you? Are you with *him*?"

"I'm not with anyone, Noah. I'm Tate. I work for the US Forest Service, and I'm here to help you." Tate shuffled into the room a few feet. "Who is he? Who locked you up?"

"That old guy. That creepy doctor. He put something over my mouth when I was walking in the woods, and next thing I knew, I was in this jail." He shook the bars, which rattled.

Tate drew closer and surveyed Noah's prison. Summers had installed a toilet and sink, a cot, an exercise bicycle. Tate's stomach turned. How long had he held the boys here? How long had he held Jeremy?

As Tate strode toward the enclosure, Noah scrambled back. Tate grabbed the padlock on the outside of the cage and asked, "Where's the key?"

"He takes it with him." Noah edged closer toward Tate. "Are you gonna get me out of here?"

"Of course I am. I told you I wasn't with Summers."

"Summers. Yeah, he keeps calling me Jackson Summers. I told him my name was Noah. I—I tried to fight him."

"I'm sure you did, son. Did Summers…hurt you?"

"Nah." Noah puffed up his chest. "Only to get me to stop yelling or trying to escape when he brings food and stuff."

Tate scanned the rest of the building for tools he could use to break the lock. He didn't want to shoot at it. Too risky. "Where is he now?"

"He went to get some girl."

Tate froze and spun around back toward the cage. "What girl? A young girl?"

"No, some lady." Noah rubbed is nose. "He came in here all mad. Sometimes he does that. Comes in here all upset and yelling and stuff. He's not even yelling at me. It's like he's yelling at the wall. Walks around and grabs his head."

"What did he say this time?" Tate grabbed the bars. "Do you remember? It's very important."

"Said some lady from the FBI was looking for me. I told him they would. Said he was gonna stop her."

"When was this, Noah?"

"Like, I don't know. Earlier today after he brought

me lunch." He aimed his toe at a tray on the floor and kicked it. "Hasn't even brought me dinner, yet."

"Do you know where he is? Where he goes?"

"Nah." He kicked the tray again, and it skittered across the cement floor. "Are you gonna let me out, or what?"

"Just hang on one minute. I saw some tools outside."

As he turned away again, Noah sniffled, his bravado seeping away. "Don't leave me here."

"I'm not going to leave you. I'll be back in a minute."

Tate ran back outside and found a pickax and a hammer. He came back inside with both, and a big grin spread across Noah's tear-stained face.

"I thought you were gone. Hey, I thought of something else he said."

"Told you I wasn't leaving." He hoisted the hammer. "Stand back."

He brought it down on the lock and hit a bar instead. The cage rattled. He tried again and got a direct hit. Two more swings and the lock broke.

Tate yanked open the door and Noah flew at him, wrapping his arms around his waist, sobs racking his thin frame. Tate thumped him on the back. "It's okay. You're okay. I'm going to take you back to your parents. But can you tell me what you remembered, first?"

Noah staggered back, his cheeks red as he ran an arm beneath his nose. "Yeah, he told me he was gonna kill that lady back in the same place where it all started. I don't know what that means, though."

"I do, Noah. I know exactly what that means."

BLANCA SHIVERED AS the rain dripped from her hood down her collar. She pulled her jacket closed at the throat.

"Why did you let Tate live all those years ago, Scotty? Why not take him or kill him?"

"Why would I kill him?" He rolled his shoulders, and the gun wavered for a second. "He didn't see me. He fell off his bike after I already had Jeremy secured. I hit him on the back of the head to make sure I could get him away from the scene and tie him up."

"And the blood in his shoes? Why were the bottoms of his feet torn up?"

"He lost his shoes when his bike crashed, and then he ran from me." Summers hardened his jaw. "Troublemaker. That's why I hit him on the head, but he never saw me. When I tied him to the tree, I went back and got his shoes. Put them back on his feet."

She narrowed her eyes. "Why not just kill him? Why go to all that trouble?"

"Ingrid." He patted his chest. "I always had a soft spot for Ingrid. I didn't want to take her boy away like mine had been taken from me."

Blanca's heart skipped a beat when she saw a light flicker in the trees behind Summers. Was someone else here? Noah? Maybe he could run for help. Porter Monroe? What she wouldn't give to have Porter crashing around the woods with his dog again.

Just when she thought she'd imagined the light, it came on again, as if in a pattern. Someone was here. Someone was listening.

"Tell me about your son, Scotty. Tell me about Jackson."

His head jerked up. "My son is with me now. I'm going to care for him. I'll convince him to stay with me like I couldn't convince Jeremy or Gabe."

"No, I mean Jackson, your five-year-old boy. Tell me about him, Scotty. Did he look like you or your wife? What was his favorite color?"

Scotty clutched his head with his free hand. "Stop. Jackson is gone now, but every seven years he's reborn in another boy. I don't want to talk about Jackson. I'm sorry I have to kill you. If you'd just left the island... Nobody cares about Jeremy Ruesler anymore. Tate doesn't care."

An eerie whistle floated out of the trees, behind Scotty. The slow "Hokey Pokey" tune wafted across the air, and Scotty staggered back against the tree, his weapon wavering at his side.

As someone came charging out of the bushes, Blanca dove for the ground and rolled away from the clearing. A gunshot blasted, the sound reverberating in her ears. Was Scotty shooting at her? She dug her fingers into the organic matter that carpeted the forest to pull herself farther along the ground behind a log.

When she heard grunting and scrabbling among the leaves, she poked up her head. Two men tussled on the ground. Her eyes, already adjusted to the dark, picked out Tate straddling Scotty, a gun to his head.

He rasped. "I should kill you. I should kill you right now for what you did to Jeremy and all those other boys."

Blanca rose to her knees. "Tate, don't. They'll get justice, thanks to you."

Sirens wailed in the distance, and Scotty bucked beneath Tate.

"That's right, Summers. I already called the police, and I already have Noah, safe in my car. He's going home to his real parents, and you're going to tell me where you buried Jeremy so I can bring him back to his family, too."

Epilogue

Birdie Ruesler wiped a tear from her cheek and hugged Tate. "I'm sorry for all those years, Tate. I'm sorry I blamed you."

Tate held Birdie's thin hands in his. "You don't have to apologize, Birdie. I understood because I blamed myself."

"I know you did, and I had no right to add to your guilt. You were a child. I was just so angry, I had to direct it somewhere. I'm ashamed it landed on you."

"You lost your son. You don't owe anyone any apologies."

"And you lost your best friend and your innocence." She patted his arm and nodded toward a dark-haired woman with a baby in her arms walking toward them. "Did you see Celine before the funeral?"

"No." He held out his hand to Jeremy's sister. "I think I would've recognized you anywhere."

She kissed his cheek. "I don't doubt it, the way you and Jeremy used to bug me and Astrid all the time. Mom's coming to live with us in Idaho. She doesn't need to wait anymore, and I need her expertise with this one."

"That's a great idea." Tate tickled the baby under the chin, and she gurgled.

"He's a natural with kids." Blanca came up behind him and put a casual hand on his shoulder.

Birdie touched Blanca's face. "Celine, this is Agent Blanca Lopez with the FBI. She's the one who helped Tate bring our Jeremy home to us."

Celine shifted her baby to the other hip. "Nice to meet you in person, Agent Lopez. I read all about you and how you were able to connect all the cases of the missing boys."

"Tate's the one who found Noah Fielding, rescued me from Summers and made him tell us where he'd buried Jeremy. If he ever gets tired of forest fires, he might have another career opportunity."

Squeezing Tate's arm, Celine said, "And Jeremy's up there smiling down at you, Tate."

Blanca took Tate's hand, and they wandered away from the rest of the mourners, who included Gabe's family, Andrew Finnigan's mother and the Fielding family, who'd returned to the island for Jeremy's funeral.

They sat together on a bench under several towering Douglas firs. The sun shifted through the branches, creating a dappled pattern across their laps.

Tate traced one of these patterns on Blanca's thigh with his fingertip. "I still can't wrap my head around the fact that Dr. Summers fed on his own grief to destroy so many other lives."

"Look at Birdie. Grief makes people react irrationally—oh, and Dr. Summers happens to be a psychopath. The point is, you brought peace to a lot of people…and indescribable happiness to the Fieldings. Noah worships you." She rubbed his back and kissed his jaw. "You also brought peace to yourself and that twelve-year-boy you used to be."

"I may have done the heavy lifting, but you're the one who thought out of the box and linked all those cases together. None of the other law enforcement officials who looked at these abductions brought the same insight that you did. You're a rock star, Blanca Lopez. Does the agency know that now?"

"I think they're catching on to my brilliance. They have an assignment for me in DC, some analyst work." She tucked her arm in his. "That means I have to go home, but there's always face-to-face on our laptops. We can get kinda kinky online."

"Yeah, about that." He pressed his lips to the side of her head. "I put in for an assignment that's going to take me to DC. Do you think you can show me around when I'm there?"

She squealed and grabbed his face with both of her hands. "No way. Are you serious? I mean, I know we talked about taking this relationship further, but I thought that was just you sweet-talking your way into my bed."

He eased out a breath, not wanting to show her how relieved he was at her response. "Ha! I told you I didn't do one-night stands, not with you."

She put her luscious mouth on his. "That's not what I heard around here. Small towns, ya know?"

"Ah, that was before. Before you helped that skinny twelve-year-old boy find peace and redemption."

She kissed him again, and he didn't feel guilty at all about his happiness. In fact, he had a feeling that Jeremy was giving him a wink.

* * * * *

*If you missed the first A Discovery Bay Novel
from Carol Ericson, look for*
Misty Hollow Massacre,
available now!

*And there are more books still
to come in this compelling series.*

#2193 COLD CASE IDENTITY
Hudson Sibling Solutions • by Nicole Helm
Palmer Hudson has a history of investigating cold case crimes. Helping his little sister's best friend, Louisa O'Brien, uncover the truth about her biological parents should be simple. But soon their investigation becomes a dangerous mystery...complicated by an attraction neither can deny.

#2194 MONSTER IN THE MARSH
The Swamp Slayings • by Carla Cassidy
When businessman Jackson Fortier meets Josie Cadieux, a woman who now lives deep in the swamp, he agrees to help find the mysterious man who assaulted her a year earlier. Soon, Josie's entry into polite upper-crust society to expose the culprit changes Jackson's role from investigator to protector.

#2195 K-9 SECURITY
New Mexico Guard Dogs • by Nichole Severn
Rescuing lone survivor Elena Navarro from a deadly cartel attack sends Cash Meyers's bodyguard instincts into overdrive. The former marine—and his trusty K-9 partner—will be damned if she falls prey a second time...even if he loses his heart keeping her safe.

#2196 HELICOPTER RESCUE
Big Sky Search and Rescue • by Danica Winters
After a series of strange disappearances, jaded helicopter pilot Casper Keller joins forces with Kristin Lauren, a mysterious woman involved in his father's death. But fighting the elements, sabotage and a mission gone astray may pale in comparison to the feelings their reluctant partnership exposes...

#2197 A STALKER'S PREY
West Investigations • by K.D. Richards
Actress Bria Baker is being stalked. And her ex, professional bodyguard Xavier Nichols, is her best hope for finishing her movie safely. With Bria's star burning as hot as her chemistry with Xavier, her stalker is convinced it's time for Bria to be his...

#2198 THE SHERIFF'S TO PROTECT
by Janice Kay Johnson
Savannah Baird has been raising her niece since her troubled brother's disappearance. But when his dead body is discovered—and unknown entities start making threats—hiding out at officer Logan Quade's isolated ranch is their only chance at survival...and her brother's only chance at justice.

YOU CAN FIND MORE INFORMATION ON UPCOMING HARLEQUIN TITLES,
FREE EXCERPTS AND MORE AT HARLEQUIN.COM.

HICNM1223

Get 3 FREE REWARDS!

We'll send you 2 FREE Books <u>plus</u> a FREE Mystery Gift.

FREE Value Over **$20**

Both the **Harlequin Intrigue®** and **Harlequin® Romantic Suspense** series feature compelling novels filled with heart-racing action-packed romance that will keep you on the edge of your seat.

YES! Please send me 2 FREE novels from the Harlequin Intrigue or Harlequin Romantic Suspense series and my FREE gift (gift is worth about $10 retail). After receiving them, if I don't wish to receive any more books, I can return the shipping statement marked "cancel." If I don't cancel, I will receive 6 brand-new Harlequin Intrigue Larger-Print books every month and be billed just $6.49 each in the U.S. or $6.99 each in Canada, a savings of at least 13% off the cover price, or 4 brand-new Harlequin Romantic Suspense books every month and be billed just $5.49 each in the U.S. or $6.24 each in Canada, a savings of at least 12% off the cover price. It's quite a bargain! Shipping and handling is just 50¢ per book in the U.S. and $1.25 per book in Canada.* I understand that accepting the 2 free books and gift places me under no obligation to buy anything. I can always return a shipment and cancel at any time by calling the number below. The free books and gift are mine to keep no matter what I decide.

Choose one: ☐ **Harlequin Intrigue Larger-Print** (199/399 BPA GRMX) ☐ **Harlequin Romantic Suspense** (240/340 BPA GRMX) ☐ **Or Try Both!** (199/399 & 240/340 BPA GRQD)

Name (please print)

Address _____ Apt. #

City _____ State/Province _____ Zip/Postal Code

Email: Please check this box ☐ if you would like to receive newsletters and promotional emails from Harlequin Enterprises ULC and its affiliates. You can unsubscribe anytime.

Mail to the Harlequin Reader Service:
IN U.S.A.: P.O. Box 1341, Buffalo, NY 14240-8531
IN CANADA: P.O. Box 603, Fort Erie, Ontario L2A 5X3

Want to try 2 free books from another series? Call 1-800-873-8635 or visit www.ReaderService.com.

*Terms and prices subject to change without notice. Prices do not include sales taxes, which will be charged (if applicable) based on your state or country of residence. Canadian residents will be charged applicable taxes. Offer not valid in Quebec. This offer is limited to one order per household. Books received may not be as shown. Not valid for current subscribers to the Harlequin Intrigue or Harlequin Romantic Suspense series. All orders subject to approval. Credit or debit balances in a customer's account(s) may be offset by any other outstanding balance owed by or to the customer. Please allow 4 to 6 weeks for delivery. Offer available while quantities last.

Your Privacy—Your information is being collected by Harlequin Enterprises ULC, operating as Harlequin Reader Service. For a complete summary of the information we collect, how we use this information and to whom it is disclosed, please visit our privacy notice located at corporate.harlequin.com/privacy-notice. From time to time we may also exchange your personal information with reputable third parties. If you wish to opt out of this sharing of your personal information, please visit readerservice.com/consumerschoice or call 1-800-873-8635. **Notice to California Residents**—Under California law, you have specific rights to control and access your data. For more information on these rights and how to exercise them, visit corporate.harlequin.com/california-privacy.

HIHRS23